I0689375

Marietta Harris

Thou

Shalt

Kill

ISBN: 978-0-996-1862-3-0

Book cover by Julie Trombley (ajulietrombley@gmail.com)

Other Books
The Other Side of Alzheimer's, a Caregiver's story
The Gospel Choir Murder – Evelyn Jenkins Series Book One

Coming Soon
A Homeless Murder
Murder by Prayer
The Red Head Girl

RBMB Publishing, 2181 N. Tracy Blvd., #208
Tracy CA 95376 (209 487-0658)
RBMB1263@yahoo.com
Printed in the United States of America

FROM THE AUTHOR

Hi. I'm Marietta Harris, the author. I get a shiver of delight whenever I say that. Ever since I was a child, I've been fascinated with the idea that a story can be manifested in an imagination, put into an order, written down, and published to impact thousands of people.

I'm a native San Franciscan who has traveled as a vocalist and musician. I lived briefly in Europe but now reside back in the San Francisco Bay Area. Years ago, after retiring, I started a new life. I finished my first book, *"The Other Side of Alzheimer's, a Caregiver's Story,"* based on my own experience caring for my mother.

After self-publishing *The Other Side of Alzheimer's,* I was invited by various groups to speak to their members who are now experiencing life as caregivers for the first time. I toured in Germany and Italy and was interviewed for a TV show in Pasadena, CA. I continue to do motivational speaking.

My favorite books have always been mysteries. My first mystery novel in the Evelyn Jenkins Series is called "The Gospel Choir Murder."

This is the second of three books in the Evelyn Jenkins Series. "Thou Shalt Kill."

You can contact me at:
Website: mariettaharris.com
Email: mariettaharris@yahoo.com

Marietta Harris

Acknowledgments

Thanks to a special friend, Carol Fairweather, for the endless hours you spent reading this manuscript. Also for the great suggestions and all the other efforts, you did to make this book possible. Carol there aren't enough words to express how much I appreciate your help. Without your input and direction, this book would not have been written.

Thank you to a wonderful lady, and editor, Buffie Peterson. Thanks for devoting your precious time and energy editing my words. I can't express how much I appreciate you assisting me in getting this book finished.
(www.facebook.com/petersonediting)

A true friend, Janice Buxton who believes in me and without your continued encouragement helps me realize my written voice is worth sharing. Words can't express how much you mean to me.

To Julie Trombley the best book designer ever. You are a wonderful and gifted lady. Thanks for helping my vision come to reality. I wish you continued blessings and can't wait to work with you in the future.
(ajulietrombley@gmail.com)

Special thanks to San Joaquin Sheriff Department.
Any mistakes with police procedures are mine.

Table of Contents

On a *Wednesday afternoon in March, the 58th Baptist Convention convened in Oakland, California.*

James Tabernacle Baptist Church hosted over 1500 members. It was their first time hosting, and Rev. Dr. Jerold Jackson was determined that this convention would surpass all others.

Anxious about the evening service scheduled for 7:00 p.m., Pastor Jackson left his wife in their hotel suite. He had to ensure all the arrangements met his expectations.

As he exited the elevator, he answered his cell. His secretary Donna spoke frantically, "Pastor Jackson, I just received a call from Pastor Jacobs' secretary. He's ill and is unable to speak tonight."

"That left only three hours to find a substitute speaker," Pastor Jackson recalled a fellow clergyman named Pastor Davenport, the youngest Senior Pastor in the Bay Area and a dynamic speaker.

"Pastor Jackson, did you hear what I said?"

"Donna, please get me the number of Pastor Gail Davenport."

Soon he was dialing. "Pastor Davenport, this is Rev. Jerald Jackson of James Tabernacle Baptist Church. How are you today?"

Clicking his cell off fifteen minutes later, Rev. Jackson exhaled deeply while Pastor Davenport sat down at his home to write a sermon on "Working together to Change the World."

Pastor Davenport would call when he arrived at the hotel valet station. Rev. Jackson's son would escort him to the room provided for guest ministers.

Rev. Jackson smiled. Adding a new pastor and church to the convention would be a feather in his cap. This was a win-win situation.

Word spread that the new speaker that evening would be the Bay Area's youngest senior pastor. At 7:00 p.m., the choir started with a powerful praise and worship. By 8:00 p.m., everyone was in place. Twenty-five ministers and pastors sat on the platform. The atmosphere in the crowded auditorium was electric.

In the large speaker's chair sat tall handsome Pastor Gail Davenport, nervous but ready. On his right was Rev. Jackson, praying the young pastor's message would suit the occasion. On Pastor Davenport's left sat the honorable Rev. Dr. Amos Moore, the President of the Convention.

When praise and worship ended, Rev. Jackson walked to the podium and proclaimed, "It's preaching time," receiving shouts of "Amen!"

Pastor Jackson continued "The Lord is truly in this place." The congregation responded. "Hallelujah."

"Isn't God good?"

"All the time," responded the congregation.

Rev. Jackson motioned to Pastor Davenport.

Point your right hand toward Pastor Davenport and repeat after me, "Preach, Pastor Davenport, Preach."

The response came. "Preach, Pastor Davenport, Preach." They clapped with excitement.

With a bible and a glass of water in hand he passed Rev. Jackson.

At the podium, Pastor Davenport looked over at the audience opened his Bible, and in a deep baritone, began to pray. Suddenly, he felt the room spin and grasped the pulpit with both hands, trying not to show his discomfort. He reached for the water on the podium with one hand and took a big gulp. His pulse raced. He wanted to loosen his tie but was afraid to take his hands off the podium. A sharp pain ripped through his chest.

The audience began murmuring.

Sweat was pouring down his face. His legs weakened. He tried to walk back to his chair, but he turned, clutched his chest and dropped, face first, to the floor.

Someone screamed. People stood trying to see what had happened. Ministers on the podium ran to his aid. They turned him over. His eyes were open. Blood gushed from his nose. His body started to shake. His chest heaved, as Pastor Davenport gasping for air until his breath stopped.

Chapter 1

Homicide Detective Alfred DeMarcus and his partner, Billy Parker are one of the youngest detectives on the Oakland Police force. They have solved over twenty cases.

Most recently, they assisted the Las Vegas Police Department in apprehending a murderer.

Evelyn Jenkins, the owner of an Oakland travel agency, had helped solve the case at Gabriel Missionary Baptist Church. Pastor Watson said she was exhausted and depressed. Alfred waited a week before asking her to come in for a deposition.

Pastor Watson left messages every day. Evelyn had nightmares the first few nights after the ordeal, but as the days passed, the bad dreams subsided. She'd lost her appetite. The only people she wanted to talk to were her family and Deborah, her assistant. Her mother wanted her to come home, but Evelyn refused.

Within a week, she started to feel like herself. Detective DeMarcus called to set up an appointment for a deposition.

Feeling stronger, she called Pastor Watson. He tried to convince her to return to church, but she didn't feel up to it.

Because the murderer had confessed, there was no need for a trial. All she had to do was give a deposition. Deborah had supported her throughout the ordeal and, because the travel agency was doing well, Evelyn had decided to stay in Oakland.

She met thirty-two-year-old Homicide Detective Alfred DeMarcus on her first visit to the Oakland Police Station. He was walking toward her wearing a black suit with a white tie. The attractive, six foot four man with a handsome bronze complexion and wavy black hair took her breath away. Their eyes met as he held out his large hand surrounding hers with an equal mix of power and softness. He was beautiful. When he said her name in a soft firm voice, she was hooked.

"Mrs. Jenkins, I'm Detective Alfred DeMarcus."

"It's Ms. Jenkins."

He smiled showing his perfectly straight white teeth. Evelyn began fidgeting as she wondered if her hair was in place.

"Thank you for coming in. We'll try and make this as short as possible."

She realized he was still holding her hand. Was Alfred feeling the same attraction? He finally let go.

"Please follow me."

She took pleasure in watching him walk in front of her. It had been months since she'd thought about dating. Starting a business consumed all of her time.

After the deposition, he asked her out for coffee, but not wanting to appear too eager, she said no.

Two days later Evelyn received a bouquet of roses at work. Alfred followed up with a call. Evelyn agreed to have dinner. She hadn't expected a relationship to develop, but that's what happened. When she opened the door on that first date, she said, "Hello," but inside her head, she was screaming, "LORD! YOU DO GOOD WORK."

On their third date, he pulled her into his arms and kissed her. He turned, smiled and said good night. Her knees buckled. She barely slept that night from excitement. That was two months ago and they still haven't consummated their relationship. They decided not to get physical before making sure their feelings were real. Evelyn didn't have time for flings, but she knew she liked him. Alfred seemed to feel the same way.

When Evelyn told her brother a police officer in Arizona, she was dating a detective he warned her. He said being married to a cop was hard and that most ended in divorce. Now she couldn't imagine breaking up with Alfred.

Even though she still wasn't going to church, her business had doubled. Pastor Watson still referred other preachers to her travel agency. His most recent recommendation was a minister from Japan. Now ministers of all denominations call her for travel assistance. Evelyn upgraded her website and was able to hire a second assistant. She promoted Deborah to office manager.

Deborah convinced Evelyn to get a vendor booth at the Baptist Convention at the Oakland Convention Center. Rev. Dr. Jackson, one of her clients, offered her a good discount. She accepted.

On Tuesday morning, Deborah and Evelyn arrived at 7:30 a.m. with signs, business cards, and brochures. The vendor's area was in a large room far from the night services. By eight, her booth was ready for business. To her surprise, there was a constant stream of people stopping at her table. Within hours, she'd passed out more than 50 business cards and received 30 cards from potential clients.

Wednesday was another good day. That night at 8:00 p.m., there were just a few customers in the vendor area. Evelyn was tired. The scheduled speaker was Rev. Jacobs Adams of New Hope Church of Christ in San Mateo CA. Evelyn thought about staying for night service but decided against it. She left. Several blocks from the hotel Evelyn heard sirens. In the rearview mirror, she saw an ambulance turn into the hotel parking lot.

Thursday morning Evelyn was shocked to hear that Rev. Gail Davenport had collapsed and died of a heart attack. Everyone was talking about it.

At 7:00 p.m. she gathered her belongings and left. Just as she arrived home, her phone rang.

"Hello, Evelyn, how are you?" She could feel her heart skip a beat.

"I'm doing well. How have you been?"

"It's been busy. I'm sorry I haven't called you." Alfred stated.

"I understand."

"I miss you." His soft, sexy voice sent shivers down her spine. She shifted in her chair and smiled.

"How about I pick you up at seven tomorrow night and take you to dinner? I can't wait to see you."

She smiled, "Sounds good; I can't wait to see you, too."

On Friday it was hard for her to concentrate. All Evelyn could think about was her date. Finding the right dress proved difficult. When her doorbell rang, she forced herself to walk, not run, to the door.

With a big smile, Evelyn opened the door. Alfred put his arms around her and kissed her. His firm body pressed against hers. Her body responded. With their faces inches apart, they stared into each other's eyes. Alfred cooed in her ear, "Hey, you."

"Hey," Evelyn softly responded, turning to retrieve her purse she hoped she wasn't drooling.

They walked hand in hand to the car.

At dinner, Evelyn told him about her experience at the convention. She was surprised to hear he had been there Wednesday night. He said when he arrived the EMT's were still trying unsuccessfully to resuscitate the pastor. A minister/doctor that was present had declared it looked like a heart attack.

The rest of the evening Alfred focused his attention on Evelyn. After dinner, he drove her home and ardently kissed her good night. It was getting harder for him to walk away and they both felt it.

Chapter 2

Saturday morning was a typically cold and foggy morning in Oakland, California. Alfred went to work early. He was always in a good mood after a date with Evelyn. With his feet on the desk, he dialed her number. Hearing his voice made her body tingle.

"Hi, I was just thinking about you." Evelyn was beaming.

"I was thinking about you, too."

"What are you up to today?"

"Well, I have a hair appointment. After that, I'm going to run some errands then get some work done. I'm cooking dinner, would you like to come over?"

"Maybe, it depends on how my day goes. I'll give you a call later."

"Don't work too hard. I'll talk with you later."

"Sounds good." He hung up and smiled.

His partner walked in. Billy Parker is 29-years-old. He was born and raised in Dallas, Texas. With his muscular body, a thick accent, blond hair, blue eyes and cowboy boots he has a way of disarming criminals during questioning. Alfred was slow and methodical. Billy was fast and liked to take chances. They decided to work Saturday to catch up with the paperwork.

"Hey, man, do you believe this weather. I can't get used to these cold mornings and warm afternoons." He said the same thing almost every day.

"Billy, you should be used to it by now."

"But it's no different in the summer. I'm used to it being 100 degrees. I can't get used to this fog." They both laughed.

Billy took off his coat, grabbed a cup of coffee, and sat down at the desk. He began working on their current case. The male victim found in a locked car with a bullet in his head. They were trying to identify him. Alfred opened up a toxicology report and was shocked. The report said the minister died from poison and not a heart attack.

"What the Hell?" Alfred shouted out loud.

A stunned Billy asked, "What's up?"

Alfred stood up as his chair fell back on the floor. He was in disbelief. He read it again. "What the Hell?" This time, he said it louder. Alfred didn't hear Billy.

"Al, what's wrong?"

"Remember that call we went to at the convention center Wednesday night? You know the preacher who they said died of a heart attack? Well, it wasn't a heart attack that killed him, it was poison."

"What?"

"The report says the poison is "undetermined."

"Man Oh Man, the preacher was murdered!"

They began reading their notes from that night. Alfred went to the whiteboard to outline the facts they had from that night. They made a list of all the ministries they spoke with, the EMT's who responded and a list of things they needed to do. Both agreed a complete autopsy was necessary. They would need a copy of the convention program to compare the names with the witness statements.

"Al, when are they supposed to bury this guy?" asked Billy.

"Man, we better find out quick, or they'll have him buried before we know it. Listen, I'll call the lieutenant and let him know we have an APE (Acute Political Emergency which means a high profile case). We've got some catching up to do, and we better do it quick." While Alfred was on the phone with the lieutenant, Billy worked on the details of the case.

"Hello, Lieutenant Rader, this is Detective Alfred DeMarcus."

"Hello, detective, why are you calling me at home?" Alfred spoke fast.

"I hate to bother you, but we have a serious problem. Remember the preacher who died at the convention? Well, I just read the toxicology report, somebody poisoned him. Billy and I are in the office working on the case. The funeral is scheduled soon. We need an autopsy. Everyone assumed he died of a heart attack. There was no autopsy. If they hadn't done a toxicology report, his death would still be considered a heart attack. Can you pull some strings? We've got to get this guy's body to the morgue. He lived in Redwood City, but I want our coroner to do the autopsy." The silence on the other end of the phone was deafening. He could hear his boss trying to absorb the nature of what he just heard.

Finally, he said, "Are you telling me this was a murder?"

"Yes, sir, this may have been going on for a while." Again, there was silence on the phone.

"Listen, I better call the mayor."

"Let me call you back. In the meantime, keep this quiet. Don't tell anybody. Is there anybody in the office with you guys?"

"No."

"Well, if anybody shows up, don't share this. I'll call you back." Click, silence.

Alfred hung up the phone, turned to Billy with a shocked look on his face.

"Man, I don't know what just happened, but we've got a high-profile case on our hands. We better find out who killed this pastor fast." Pouring himself a cup of coffee, Alfred though, this is going to be a long day. Twenty minutes later the phone rang, it was Lieutenant Radar.

"Detective, I just spoke with the mayor. You and Billy are assigned this case. Whatever you need, come to me, nobody else. I'll contact Redwood City Police and tell them what we have. They may have some information that can solve this case. They will assist you locally. If anybody asks, refer them to me. For now, you and Billy can take the office in the back room. If there's no lock on the door, get one. You're going to be talking to some high-level people. Preachers don't like talking to the police. Be polite, but don't take any shit, and don't tell them anything. I'll call the family to get permission to do an autopsy before the funeral. Call the coroner and make sure he's available tomorrow. Tell him this is top-priority. I need that report on my desk no later than Monday. If reporters get wind of this, all hell's going to break. Have you made a list of who you talked to that night? You need to speak with them again."

"No, we're just getting started on it."

"Well, get to it, most of these ministers have already left town. You need to do interviews. Get started on that yesterday." Lieutenant yelled.

"We will."

As he hung up the phone, Alfred got a knot in his stomach.

"This is going to be big."

"Back home, preachers don't get poisoned. Man, I can't ever remember a pastor getting killed."

"Billy, welcome to city life. Lieutenant Radar said we need to move to that room in the back. We don't report to anyone but him. Reporters will be all over this." Alfred asked,

"Is there a lock on that room in the back?"

"I don't know I'll check." Billy went to check, and Alfred started gathering up files and notes. They moved the white board, chairs, and a table into the back room and had the locks changed.

Billy read the report from the first officer on the scene. He called Officer David Glenn and asked him to come to the office. He agreed. Billy hoped Officer Glenn could provide additional information.

They matched business cards with names. Officer Glenn arrived an hour later. Not wanting to indicate the seriousness of the crime, Billy said he read his report and wanted to get his impression of the scene.

"Well, we received a call of a serious incident at the hotel. My partner and I were the first on the scene. When we arrived, people were running around screaming and saying they needed an ambulance. Within minutes, the ambulance arrived. We found an African-American man, who was identified as a Rev. Gail Davenport, lying on the floor. He appeared unconscious. A man identified himself as a Rev. Jones approached and said the minister fell unconscious just before he was to preach. We saw another minister who said he was a doctor performing CPR. We got the names of the people who were in the room. The other witnesses said the same thing. The EMT continued to try to resuscitate him. They did chest compression and put a breathing apparatus on him. That continued while they put him on a gurney and placed him into the ambulance.

"Did anything appear to be suspicious?" Billy asked.

"Suspicious! Suspicious how?"

"Was there anybody in the room that should not have been there?" "Was anyone talking negatively about the minister?"

"No, not really but it's hard to say. Most of the people in there were ministers. One of the EMT's said he believed it was a heart attack just like the doctor said."

"Officer, I'm looking through the report, but I don't see the names of the people who were in the room."

"When we found out the guy died of a heart attack I didn't think it was important enough to add it to my report. I can email it to you." Billy didn't want to make it sound like it was critical, but it was.

"It would be helpful if you can. Listen, thanks for coming in."

"No problem. That was my first emergency at a convention. The minister died in route to the hospital." Billy gave him a business card with his email address on it, shook his hand, and showed him the way out.

It was four o'clock p.m. before they matched up business cards with the names of ministers. Realizing they hadn't eaten, they ordered pizza.

An hour and a half later, Alfred's cell phone rang. It was Evelyn. She wanted to know if he was still coming for dinner.

"Hello, Alfred."

"Hello Evelyn, what are you doing?"

"I'm just leaving the hair salon. I called to find out how your day was and if you're still planning on coming to dinner."

Alfred paused. He knew this case was going to consume every bit of his time. Tonight might be a good opportunity to relax. It may be a long time before he gets to see her again.

Because there was a long pause, Evelyn felt guilty as if she was interfering with his job.

"Listen, if you can't make it, it's all right."

"That's not it. Yes, I'll be at your place around seven is that a good time for you?"

"Are you sure?"

He changed his voice to sound more relaxed. "Yes, Yes I'll be there. I can't wait to see you. Should I bring anything?"

"No," He smiled.

"I'll be there with bells on." They hung up.

"Is that your girl?" Billy asked.

"Yes, someday I'll introduce you to her. This case is going to be a challenge. I figure this is the last night I'll get a chance to see her for a while. Are you seeing someone?"

"Well, I'm dating this beautiful lady. I'm not serious, but I like her."

"Well, I suggest you see her tonight because this case is going to take the majority of our time." Billy shrugged his shoulders, stood up, walked out the office, and made a call. Alfred smiled. They finished around 6:30 p.m. and decided to meet back at 7 a.m.

This case could change their careers. Alfred thought about his childhood. His parents were devout Catholics. Growing up, he was forced to attend church every day. On Sundays, all his friends went to their church. After he had graduated from college, he stopped attending church.

Like Alfred, Billy was thinking about his religious experience growing up. In Texas, all the kids played together. Blacks, Hispanics, Jews, it didn't matter. His parents belonged to the Church of Christ. Like Alfred, on Sundays, everybody attended their church. He liked going because they had a youth church. He stopped going to church when he grew up.

Since Evelyn's dad was a pastor, Alfred knew she could tell him what happens in the African-American churches.

When Evelyn answered the door, he grabbed her by the waist and pulled her body close to his. They kissed. He could feel the heat between them. Evelyn wasn't used to this. She moaned but slowly put her arms down to her side. He let go, reached down, grabbed his briefcase and followed her into the living room. Evelyn knew she was sending mixed signals. One minute she wanted him to make love to her but she was scared of giving in to her emotions.

Evelyn turned and smiled, "You must have had a busy day."

Alfred was confused. Now he wasn't sure if she felt the same way he did.

"Well, I expect it will get busier in the coming days."

"I hope you're hungry."

"I sure am." He chuckled. He could hear her laughing in the kitchen. Alfred washed his hands, ready to eat. They ate. After dinner, he found himself in deep in thought.

"So what new cases are you working on?" Alfred didn't answer so she asked him again. "Alfred!" Suddenly he realized he hadn't heard a word she said.

"It's going to be a real high profile case, but I can't talk about it now."

"That's all right. I understand." Evelyn began telling him about her day, but he wasn't listening. He decided Evelyn could help him. He wouldn't tell her everything, but she could share some insight as to how conventions work.

"That sounds great. What happens at these conventions?"

"You want to know?"

"Yes, so who decides who's going to preach during these nights services?"

"I don't know, but I can find out if you want. What's this all about?" Alfred didn't want to go any further, but he knew once the investigation started, Evelyn would know he was involved. He trusted her, and she could help him understand the workings of the convention. He paused,

"Evelyn, I'm not supposed to tell anyone, but remember that minister who everyone thinks died of a heart attack? Well, someone poisoned him." Evelyn gasped as her face paled. He could see the shock on her face.

"Billy and I are going to start our field investigation tomorrow. Lieutenant Rader wants to keep it hush-hush, but I suspect once we start interrogating the ministers, I'm going to be busy."

Before he finished talking, Evelyn had sat down at the table. "Pastor Davenport was murdered?" She could feel her body starting to shake. She couldn't believe her ears. Murder! Alfred suddenly realized how she must feel. After all, it's only been two months since she was involved with murder. He hugged her and apologized.

"Evelyn, I'm sorry I didn't realize how this would affect you."

Evelyn couldn't say a word. He poured her a glass of water and waited for her to respond. She took a gulp and put the glass down.

"Evelyn, I didn't know how this was going to affect you, especially since you were involved in a murder just months ago. I know the last thing you want to do is get involved in a murder case again."

So many thoughts were running through her brain. But the fact that she was there that night made her want to get involved. She wanted to help. Alfred was staring at her trying to decide what to say. She took a deep breath, sat back on the chair, looked at his face and said, "How can I help?" The look on her face convinced him she was serious.

"Are you sure about this?"

"Yes, I'm sure. I'm stronger than you think. Why would anybody poison a minister?"

"That's what most people will ask."

Evelyn told him everything she knew about the convention.

She could feel the adrenaline rush. It surprised her. Was this her calling? Alfred was concerned, but the expression on her face gave him the assurance she could handle the challenge. Alfred was relieved. He didn't like keeping secrets from her.

Alfred took notes. This information gave him an outline of what happened. Now he had to find out who wanted this pastor dead and why. It was almost eleven o'clock when they finished.

"Listen, you gave me some excellent information. I've got to find out who killed this guy. You can't discuss this with anyone. I'm leaving so I can get an early start tomorrow." Wrapping her arms around him, she stared into his eyes.

"Please be careful. Whoever this is is dangerous. To kill a minister is personal."

"I know."

He gave her a kiss, gathered his papers and left.

After showering, she eased her body between the clean sheets thinking next time she would invite him to her bed.

Chapter 3

Early Sunday morning Evelyn's phone rang.

She heard a soft and sexy voice, "Good morning."

"Good morning."

"Did you sleep well?"

"Yes, I wish you were here." As soon as she said it out loud, she felt embarrassed.

Alfred was shocked but thrilled. "I'll remember that the next time I come over." Evelyn laughed while propping herself up in bed looking outside.

"It's a cold and damp day. So what are you going to do today?" Alfred asked.

"I don't have any plans. I may catch up on some paperwork or just relax."

"That sounds good. I better get up and get going. I told Billy I would meet him in the office at seven. I'll be busy, so it may be a while before I see you. But I'll call." Evelyn smiled.

"I understand. Let me know if you need anything." She was glad to help.

"Believe me; I'll be thinking about you more than you'll ever know." She chuckled.

"That's good to hear," She tried sounding sexy.

"Do you have time to eat breakfast?"

"No, I'll grab a breakfast sandwich and coffee near the office. Talk to you later."

He hung up, dressed and walked into the office at 7:30.

"Hey, partner. Glad to see you," Billy greeted him sarcastically.

"Sorry to be late."

"How was your evening?"

"It was nice." He pulled out his notebook and started writing on the board.

"It must have been nice since you're not talking." Alfred chuckled. Even though Billy was his partner he kept his personal life private. Billy watched in anticipation. When he finished, Billy looked amazed.

"Where did you get this information?"

"I've got my sources."

"This looks good. It gives us a time frame to work with."

If he was a stand-in, who was scheduled to preach that night? What's his status in the convention? He must be high up on the totem pole."

"I don't know, but that's what we've got to find out." Looking over the list of ministers they decided to start with the ones in town. Using the business cards, they put them in the order they wanted to conduct the interviews.

The phone rang, and Billy answered. It was the District Attorney. As soon as he identified himself, Billy put the call on speaker.

"Can you both hear me?"

"Yes," they responded in unison.

"The mayor gave me a head's up regarding the investigation. If you need my assistance, call me directly. He wants to make sure this case doesn't get out of hand, especially because the Minister's Union is going to be all over this.

"What Minister's Union? I didn't know they had a union," Alfred interrupted.

"Yes, they have what they call a union. Ministers in the area meet once a month. Sometimes they have revivals, food drives and things like that. They're very active. You may need to talk with them. I don't know who attended the convention, but it might save you some time. Be careful talking to these guys. We don't want to make any accusations without substantial evidence. For now, you're just trying to get information to help close the case. Have you run a background check on the minister that died?"

"No, we plan on doing that today."

"The mayor talked to the wife so check her out. Find out what's going on with this guy. How long has he been here? What's going on at his church? How long has he been a member of the convention? I need you to find out everything about him. You know the drill."

"We'll get right on it."

"Let me know what you find. Somebody from Davenport's church could have poisoned him. I would start with that first. Keep me in the loop. I agree with Lieutenant Radar; we need to conduct this investigation as quite as possible." Alfred responded.

"We'll let you know what we find."

"Rader seems to think you two are the ones that can solve this case. I hope he's right because this will be a big mess if you screw it up. I'll talk to you later, bye." The phone went dead. Billy's face was red.

"Man, what did we do to deserve this? I've never heard of a minister's union."

"Billy, we can do this. Let's pull up a background check on the Davenports. Come to think about it; we have nothing on the wife." Billy looked on the board and said, "You're right."

"Damn, how did we miss that?" Billy turned to the computer and did a background check on the Davenports. Alfred looked back over his notes and noticed there was no mention of a wife that night.

Within a few minutes, Billy had Gail Davenport's information on the screen. He started telling Alfred what he found.

Gail Davenport was 30, born June 10, 1979, in San Jose CA to Thurston and Rose Davenport. He graduated from Harvard in 2006 with a degree in computer technology. Gail was a pilot with United Airlines. In 2008 he graduated from seminary school. In 2009 he married 28-year-old Yolanda Morris and was appointed Senior Pastor at Mount Jordan Baptist Church of Redwood City. They don't have any kids.

His father's a minister and realtor. The mother is a housewife. They live in Santa Clara."

These people were millionaires. Neither one had a criminal record. Alfred could see why they live in such a wealthy neighborhood.

"So he's only been married for a little over year. What about the wife?"

"Yolanda Morris Davenport is a twin.

Their parents are Troy and Vivian Morris of Tulsa Oklahoma. They moved to Santa Clara CA in 1980 and owned several dry cleaners. The mother's a housewife.

Ray and Yolanda are their only kids. They grew up in Santa Clara. Both graduated from Harvard. Yolanda's major was art. Ray graduated in Liberal Arts. Neither one has a criminal record."

"How about we start with the parents, then the wife? Is there an address for them?"

"Yes, the parents are in Santa Clara and the wife is in Redwood Shores. Let's get started."

They grabbed their coats and headed for the door. During the ride, Billy made a list of the ministers in the area. They didn't want to go to a church during service but if they had to, they would. He called the wife's parents but learned they were not at home. The Davenport's were also not home. The mother was in the hospital. He called Davenport's wife.

"Hello."

"Hello, is this Mrs. Yolanda Davenport?"

"No, this is the maid."

"Well, my name is Detective Billy Parker. Is Mrs. Davenport, there?"

"Yes, hold please." After a long moment of silence, a soft, female voice came across the line.

"Hello, this is Mrs. Davenport."

"Hello, Mrs. Davenport, my name is Detective Billy Parker with the Oakland Police Department. I'm sorry for your loss. I need to speak with you in person. We're in Redwood City and would like to come by and talk with you. Would that be okay?"

"Is there anything wrong, officer?"

"Well, ma'am, we just need to speak to you. Would that be all right with you?"

"Yes, that would be okay," She stated after a long pause.

"We'll be there shortly."

"I look forward to seeing you."

Billy hung up the phone.

"How did she sound?" Alfred asked.

"Curious. It's hard to tell on the phone."

"Well, I think we should gather as much information as we can without telling her about the poison. We'll hold off on that information for later. What do you think?"

"I agree. Why scare her if we don't have to." They rode the rest of the way in silence.

Chapter 4

Exiting the freeway they drove several blocks, turned, and entered the Palermo Estates. The guard directed them to the house. The road leads them into the driveway of the property. It was a luxurious mansion. Billy and Alfred were surprised. They parked and walked toward the front door. Facing them were two large front doors. Alfred rang the doorbell. The maid came to the door.

"May I help you?"

"Yes, my name is Detective DeMarcus, and this is my partner, Detective Parker. We're here to see Mrs. Davenport."

"She's expecting you, come in." She ushered them into a large foyer. Facing them were two staircases on each side of the wall with an oversized round table with flowers, positioned between them. To the right appeared to be in a large living room. To the left, it looked like an office with French doors. Mrs. Davenport descended the stairs on the right. She was a beautiful African-American woman about 5'6" tall wearing a very expensive black suit. The woman wore high heels, and her hair was tied back in a ponytail. They couldn't help notice she was a classy lady. She held out her hand and introduced herself; it was small and sweaty.

"Gentlemen, I'm Mrs. Davenport. Are you the officers that called earlier?"

"Yes, I'm Detective DeMarcus, and this is my partner, Detective Parker. Thank you for seeing us on such short notice. We're sorry for your loss. We just need some information to help close this case." Mrs. Davenport ushered them in the living room. Alfred sat on an overstuffed, leather couch. In front of them was a grand marble table and underneath, was a black and white rug. She sat in a wing chair facing them in front of the fireplace.

"I just can't believe this. Gail never complained about having heart pain. I just don't understand. Do you always investigate heart attacks?"

"Not always, but your husband was a prominent man in the community. We want to make sure everything is in order." It was clear she'd been crying.

Billy walked around looking at pictures on the black grand piano. Over the fireplace hung a large portrait of Gail Davenport in a robe holding a bible.

"Would you mind if I tape our conversation? I want to make sure I have everything I need to close this case."

"I don't mind." Alfred pulled out a small tape recorder and placed it on the table.

"How was your relationship?"

"Gail was the love of my life. We met at Harvard and dated for about six months before he proposed. My parents loved him the first time they met. He was intelligent, kind, and gentle. His grandfather was a preacher. Preaching was a gift. When he spoke, it was mesmerizing. I loved watching him preach. He was the happiest when he preached." It was clear she loved her husband. Tears began running down her face.

"Mrs. Davenport, were you at the convention last week?"

"No, I was in New York. I own an art gallery in San Francisco. I was there to purchase some new art pieces. Gail called me all excited and told me Pastor Jackson asked him to speak that night. Pastor Jordan took ill. We married just over a year ago. He was appointed the Senior Pastor a few months later."

"What time did he call you?"

"It was around 1:00 p.m. My husband was a great man." She pulled out a handkerchief from her sleeve and began wiping her face. The sincerity in her face was evident.

"Ma'am, did your husband have any health issues?" Alfred asked after a pause.

"No, Gail was in perfect health. He ran every morning and wouldn't eat junk food. He was constantly saying the body is a temple of God. I used to tease him about it, that's what makes this so crazy, how could he die of a heart attack?"

"Are you and your husband the only ones living here?"

"Yes, along with the help. There's Doris our live-in maid, Alisa the housekeeper, and the groundskeepers; that's it. I suppose you're wondering why we live in such a large house? Gail said we could fill it with lots of children. That's the kind of man he was." Tears continued to roll down her face. Billy sat down on the couch.

"Gentlemen, he was a pilot as well as a Pastor."

"Mrs. Davenport, do you cook?"

"Sometimes but our schedules are so full, most of the time Doris cooks, or we go out to eat."

"What type of food did he eat?"

"Well, he never ate fast food or foods with chemicals in it. He loved fresh vegetables. And every day he made this drink after running. It was a horrible concoction of orange juice, flaxseed, yogurt, and spinach. I hated it. Why are you asking me what my husband ate?"

They ignored her question.

"Did your husband have any enemies that you are aware of?"

"I don't know if you can say they were enemies, but when he became the senior pastor, not everyone in the church was happy. You know how people are. The older members wanted another ministry, and they fought hard for him."

"Are they still members of your church?"

"Some left with Pastor Warren. He started a church not far from ours. Gail tried to make everyone happy, but it just wasn't to be."

"Do you know the first name of Pastor Warren?"

"Yes, it's Jesse Warren. He was at Mount Jordan for years. I believe he expected to be the Senior Pastor, but my husband was selected. The congregation has grown so large that we have two services on Sunday. The first service is at eight and the second at eleven. He was starting a building fund drive to build a new church." She began crying harder as the maid came in.

"Gentlemen, I think Mrs. Davenport needs to rest." With the aid of the maid, Mrs. Davenport got up and left the room. Her tears had turned into sobs.

Watching her walk up the stairs, alone and in pain, Billy and Alfred felt empathy for her. The maid ushered them to the front door. Billy began to question her.

"May I ask how long have you worked for the Davenports?"

"I've been with the Davenports for over a year, ever since they moved here."

"May I ask, what is your name?" Doris was a little apprehensive about answering.

"Doris Ackers."

"Well, Ms. Ackers do you know of anyone who would want to harm Pastor Davenport?"

"No, everybody loved him. I thought they said he died of a heart attack? I know it's all in God's hands but Mrs. Davenport is taking his death hard. Did he die of a heart attack?"

"Ma'am, that's what we're investigating."

"I've never seen them argue. They truly were soul mates."

"Can you tell me Alisa last name?"

"Alisa Hernandez. She works Mondays, Wednesdays, and Fridays."

"Thank you so much. If Mrs. Davenport needs anything, here is my card, have her call me."

They took another look around turned and walked out the door.

Neither one of them said anything until they reached the car. Looking around the neighborhood, they knew this case was even bigger than they feared.

In the car, Billy took a deep breath.

"Man that was intense."

"I'll say." Alfred responded.

"Did you see her? I mean this woman is a class act. Wonder what the husband was like?" Alfred asked Billy to check the system for Doris Acker.

"She's clean no warrants or aliases." What about Alisa Hernandez.

"Nothing, she's clean." Billy checked Rev. Jesse Warren. He had no criminal record.

"Well, that's great, said Alfred. We need to talk to Rev. Warren. If he's got a new church, find the address."

Chapter 5

Billy called the church.

"Hello, Morning Side Baptist Church."

"Hello, my name is Detective Parker, is Rev. Warren there."

"Yes, he's in his office, hold on." Billy waited. Alfred started the car and headed for the church.

"Hello, this is Rev. Warren."

"Hello, Rev. Warren, my name is Detective Billy Parker. My partner and I would like to speak with you about Rev. Davenport." There was silence on the phone.

"Well, I'm in church now."

"I understand. We're just minutes away. Do you have time to speak with us?"

"Yes, I guess so. When you get here, have one of the ushers bring you to my office."

"Thank you so much. See you in a few minutes."

Within 10 minutes, they were driving into strip mall shopping center. No signs were identifying a church, just an office space with the windows covered. Alfred parked the car. He changed the recording tape and put it in his pocket. This time, Billy would do the questioning. Billy was muscular, so just his appearance was threatening.

When the door opened, you could smell the odor of a musty building. Standing inside the front door was a young girl wearing a white shirt and dark skirt. She wore a badge that said, "Usher." Not wanting to cause any attention, Billy told her Pastor Warren was expecting them. She smiled and asked them to follow her. They walked along the wall past the roll of wooden chairs with about 50 members in attendance. There was a wooden podium in front. Next to it was a portable piano. Drums were behind it. Past the curtains was a door with a sign which read office. The young lady knocked and heard a voice say, "Come In."

When the door opened, they were face to face with an older man. He was 5'9" tall, stocky with graying hair. He wore an old robe. The young lady turned and left.

"Gentlemen, come in." They shook hands.

He pointed to two cushioned chairs placed in front of a table. A table light was the only thing lighting the room. They sat down. Alfred began introductions.

"Pastor Warren, my name is Detective DeMarcus, and this is my partner, Detective Parker. We're here to gather information about Pastor Davenport." Warren's shoulders slumped as he sat back in his office chair looking shocked.

"I was sorry to hear of his untimely death. What is this all about?"

"Would you mind if we record this conversation for our records?" Warren paused in thought, finally stating, "I don't know. I guess so."

"What kind of person was he?" Billy asked.

"He was a good speaker and an intelligent, good looking, young man. Everybody liked him. I liked him."

"Did he have any health issues?"

"No, but we weren't that close. He jogged. The only thing I've seen him eat is cake at celebrations and potlucks. Members are very upset at his passing. I can't imagine what's going to happen at Mount Jordan."

"Do you know of any enemies he may have had?"

"ENEMIES, NO! I certainly wasn't an enemy. I mean we had our differences, but that's what preachers do. I have my church now." The detectives took note of his comments.

"When did you speak with him last?" Pastor Warren looked puzzled.

"I haven't talked to him for almost a year."

"Is there some reason why you didn't speak to him?" Alfred asked.

"I had no reason."

"So, there are no enemies that you know of?"

"No, and I can't think of anyone. Why are you asking?" Billy interrupted and said,

"Are you attending the funeral?"

"No!" Warren firmly replied. They stood up.

"If you think of anyone that may have had a grudge, please give me a call." Billy handed him a business card. "Thank you for your time." They shook hands and left. Billy looked at his watch: 11:10 a.m. There were a few members that stared at them as they left. An elderly lady was playing the piano, and a young boy was beating the drums. A young man was talking at the podium.

Only when they got in the car did Billy speak.

"Man, that guy has issues.

"Can you believe he's a preacher with that much hatred?"

"Al, I don't get it."

"Billy, all of them aren't like him. Listen, Mount Jordan isn't far from here, let's go by there." Billy agreed. This time, he drove.

Chapter 6

Mount Jordan was a stark contrast to the church they left. The church covered half the block. The parking lot covered the other half. Members were going in or coming out of the building. The majority of people were dressed in dark attire and consoling each other. It was busy but orderly.

They parked a block away. Walking toward the church, they overheard bits of conversations from members who expressed remorse over the death of their pastor. The church was an old regal Catholic church, with 50 foot stained glass windows. Steps were leading up to the giant front doors. Having two services explained the bustling people going in and out of the foyer. Inside to the right was a table labeled information. To the left was a small coffee shop. Facing them were several doors leading into the sanctuary. Billy was dumbfounded. The membership consisted of people of all races. Alfred opened the doors only to find a young man stationed on the other side. He was wearing a black suit and badge that identified him as an usher.

Not wanting to make a scene Alfred flashed his badge and asked to be directed to the Pastor's office. With a somber look on his face, the young man turned and spoke.

"Sir, our pastor passed away last week."

"I'm so sorry for your loss. Can we speak to the person in charge?"

"That's Pastor Nelson. He's in his office. Follow me."

Billy and Alfred followed him down the left aisle of the church. It was a powerful scene. The church was almost full. There were organs on the right side and a grand piano on the left. The pulpit chairs were purple except for one large gold chair with a black sheet draped over it. Flowers lined the podium and church. The smell was overwhelming.

The young man led them through a door and down a long wide hallway. Office signs lined the hall. He stopped at the door marked Assistant Pastor and knocked.

A voice asked, "Who is it?"

"Derik."

"Come in, Derik."

"Reverend Nelson, these policemen asked to see you." He stood up, walked around his desk, and held out his hand."

"Hello, I'm Rev. Myron Nelson. Thank you, Derik, I'll see you later."

"You're welcome." He left.

"Reverend Nelson, my name is Detective DeMarcus, and this is my partner, Detective Parker. Thank you for seeing us. We're doing a follow-up on the death of Pastor Davenport."

Rev. Nelson was a tall, husky, six-foot man with slumped shoulders. His mustache was speckled with gray and his face looked worn.

Billy began walking around the office. The room was large with a small bathroom and a closet to the right. There were two cushioned chairs in front of the desk. Pictures of Nelson and Pastor Davenport hung on the wall. Nelson motioned to the chairs, "Please have a seat." Alfred sat down.

His voice was soft and slow. "We are devastated. Pastor Davenport was a great man. We will miss him. He was a visionary, and I don't know what we're going to do."

"Are you in charge?" Billy interrupted.

"Yes, I know he would want us to go on, but it's going to be so hard. Sister Davenport is taking his death hard. They were a loving couple. I don't know if she'll make it through the funeral. Our congregation is so large that we can't have the funeral here." Alfred asked.

"Where will the funeral be held?"

"Rev. Dr. Amos Morgan of True Vine COGIC in San Mateo offered his church. They can seat at least 2,500 people. It's going to be tight, but it's the best we can do. We have dignitaries, pastors, and churches asking to participate. We want to send him off with dignity and respect."

"Did he have any enemies?"

"ENEMIES?" his voice raised. "No! He was a kind soul that everybody loved."

"When was the last time you spoke to him?"

It was evident he was trying to compose himself. After a long pause, his voice softened.

"The last time I saw him was Monday night. He had a meeting with the pastoral staff. It was a weekly event. Pastor Davenport had one of our members serve the food. We discussed plans for the week and the building of a new sanctuary. He was excited."

"May I ask who catered the food?"

"Sister Davis donated trays of fruit, sandwiches, and sodas."

"Did everyone eat at this event?"

"Yes, Pastor seemed to enjoy the food. Usually, he doesn't eat. He likes to mingle with the members, but at our meeting, he ate with us."

"I understand he worked, how often was he here at the church?"

"He worked, but he was here every Monday and sometimes during the week. He was always back by Friday for Bible study."

"Can we see his office?"

Pastor Nelson was perplexed but finally said, "Yes, of course."

"We just want to get an idea of what it looks like."

He stood up, and they followed. People were walking and talking down the halls. Someone stopped Pastor Nelson and asked him to confirm the time for the funeral service. He told them it was at 11:00 a.m. on Friday.

When they reached the stairs, he slowed down. He removed the black cord from across the stairway.

He opened the door. Soft religious music was playing. It was a sizeable room with pale purple walls. A beautiful desk stood in the middle of the room. The décor was exquisite. A portrait of the pastor and his wife was on the wall. They stood in silence. It was as if his spirit was in the room. Pastor Nelson was visibly uncomfortable. After a few seconds, he quietly spoke.

"Gentlemen, I need to get service started." Rev. Nelson locked the door and followed them downstairs.

"Rev. Nelson, thank you. We have an idea who Pastor Davenport was. It is apparent he was loved. Again, we are sorry for your loss."

"Thank you, detectives, I know you have to do your job, and I appreciate that. Will you be attending the services?"

"I don't know. If we need anything else can we call you?" Alfred gave him his business card.

"Call me anytime. But I'm going to be very busy."

"We understand. Goodbye." He pointed them to the exit.

Reverend Nelson turned and walked away. Billy and Alfred opened the ornate door to the sanctuary. It was a dramatic sight. Every seat in the church was full. Members of all races were solemnly facing the front and listening to a group of singers standing across the pulpit area. Billy stopped, turned to Alfred, and gestured that he wanted to sit down. They sat in the last row.

People continued to arrive. Within minutes, the doors closed. It was evident everyone was sad. Just as the detectives were ready to leave, they heard a conversation from two ladies standing behind them.

"Do you believe this? You'd swear he was a god or something."

"Well, he wasn't no god. I couldn't stand him. Always acting like he was better than us. Wonder if Warren's going to try and come back?"

"Girl, I doubt it. You know Rev. Warren is old school and don't like trouble. He couldn't handle these people. Are you going to the funeral?"

"Hell yea. I want to see how the misses is going to act." They were snickering.

An usher approached them, "Ladies, please follow me." They walked pass the detectives down the aisle. The conversation caught Billy and Alfred's attention. Without saying a word, they knew they had to find out who these women were. You couldn't help noticing them. Billy nudged Alfred in his side. Just as they were getting ready to leave, they overheard two women,

"Do you believe them heifers? I wish they went with Warren."

"Pastor Davenport will be missed." Another woman said.

Billy and Alfred waited a few minutes before they got up and left. Outside the building, members were still trying to get inside the sanctuary. As they exited a woman dressed similarly to the sisters was coming up the stairs.

The Detectives looked at each other and smiled. Alfred said,

"She's got to be with the other two," Billy chuckled.

"Do you believe that?"

Alfred laughed. "Man, that's the worst thing I've ever seen. They must be the talk of the church?"

"We have got to find out who they are. Before he could finish, he heard a woman behind them talking.

"Oh, God, the Johnson sisters are in the house."

They continued walking but remembered the names.

"Billy, let's go back to the office."

"That sounds good to me. Let's get lunch." That's one of the things Alfred liked about his partner. Working with Billy was easy. He never hesitated to say what he was thinking, and Alfred liked that about him.

Chapter 7

In the office, they ate lunch while listening to the message from Mrs. Davenport asking about a call from the funeral home. It seemed genuine, but they weren't ready to rule her out as a suspect.

Billy was about to call the coroner's office to see if they had the body when the phone rang.

"Hello, this is Detective DeMarcus."

"Detective DeMarcus, this is Mrs. Davenport. I received a call from the funeral home telling me the coroner requested my husband's body. Why do you need my husband's body? What's going on?" She was angry.

He knew Lieutenant Radar said he would tell her. "Mrs. Davenport I'm sorry this has caused you additional stress." He couldn't tell her the real reason.

"Please let me call my boss. I'll call you back." Without saying another word, she hung up.

Alfred was pissed. He called Lieutenant Radar. "I thought you talked to Mrs. Davenport? She just called me upset."

"Oh HELL, I forgot. Ben, the coroner, said he'd tell me when he picked up the body from the funeral home. The funeral director must have called her. Let me fix this. I'll call her right now. I talked to Lieutenant Morse in Redwood City. He assigned Detective Kiefer to help you."

The phone went dead. Alfred was relieved. The fewer people who knew about this, the better they could gather evidence. People shut down once the police get involved. Pastor Jackson was next on the list.

Billy was talking on the phone. Alfred gestured to him to cut the call by pretending to cut his throat using his index finger.

"What's up?" Alfred told him what happened. Billy called Detective Kiefer and asked for information on the Davenports, Rev. Nelson, and Rev. Warren. Kiefer promised to call back. Next on the list was Rev. Jackson.

They reached James Tabernacle Church within ten minutes. The parking lot was full. The parking director told them to park in the Pastor's wife spot. He said service was ending and pointed them to the back door. An usher greeted them and gave them a church program. They followed her to a seat. The church was full.

Chapter 8

James Tabernacle was a well-established old church. It was predominately African-American except for a few Caucasian members. Rev. Dr. Jackson, a well-groomed tall, thin man was standing at the podium. He was wearing glasses and a white robe. They recognized him from Wednesday night. He was talking about the week activities and encouraged the congregation to attend. Everyone stood for the benediction. The parking director asked them to follow him to the Pastor's study. He knocked on the door and heard, "Come in."

Pastor Jackson's office was smaller than Pastor Davenport's office. Pastor Jackson entered the room from what appeared to have been a dressing room or bathroom. He was wearing a black suit. After shaking hand, Alfred sat down while Billy perused the office.

"Aren't you the two detectives I met Wednesday night?"

"Yes, we are. I'm Detective DeMarcus, and this is my partner Detective Parker."

"How can I help you?"

"Pastor, we're doing a follow-up. As I understand it, Wednesday night was the first time you met Pastor Davenport?"

"That's correct. Pastor Davenport was Pastor Jacob's replacement. It was the first time I spoke with him."

"Were the guest speakers allowed any special privileges?"

"Well, I don't know if you call it privileges, but we treat them special. We provided Pastor Davenport a parking space and he stayed in a suite reserved for the ministers. I can't believe such a young man would die of a heart attack. No one remembered him complaining of being ill."

"Did you provide food and drinks?"

"Yes, the hotel offered catering and drinks for the entire week just for that suite."

"So food and drinks came from the hotel?"

"Some of it did. Members of my church donated drinks, cakes, and pies to help defray the cost."

"So this was open to all ministers?"

"Yes, they pop in during the day to grab a snack or drink."

"Rev. Jackson, I noticed there were drinks in the area where the ministers were sitting, is that normal?" Billy asked.

"Yes. The ladies of our church donated drinks, glasses, and water. In our community, it's okay to have water in the pulpit area."

"Why are you concerned about the drinks and food?" Alfred responded.

"We're just trying to cover all areas of our investigation."

"Why is there an investigation? Pastor Davenport died of a heart attack."

"Pastor Davenport was a remarkable man. We want to make sure there was no foul play. I'm sure you can understand. An important person like you would want us to be thorough." After a pause, Rev. Jackson said,

"Yes, yes I get it."

"Do you know if Pastor Davenport had any enemies?"

"Pastor Warren and some of the members left. I'm not sure if he had enemies. Why do you ask?" Ignoring the question Billy continued.

"Were there others who had a grudge against him?"

"Some ministers didn't like how it happened, but they wouldn't have harmed him. Things like that happen."

"So this is not the first time a church split?"

"No, I'm afraid it's not. Some member's stay, others move on."

"So some of his members might even be members of your church?"

"Yes, that can happen."

"When they join, do they say what church they're from?"

"Yes, it's called Christian experience, which means they've been a member of another church."

"Well, thank you for your time. We don't want to hold you any longer. Will you be attending the funeral services?"

"Yes, I will. I've been asked to read scripture. Sister Davenport is taking his death hard."

Billy and Alfred stood up, shook hands, gave him a business card and walked out. Rev. Jackson felt this investigation was unusual.

The sanctuary was empty. It was an eerie feeling.

"Al, are you thinking what I'm thinking? Some people may have wanted Davenport dead."

"I agree. Let's get back and make a list."

Chapter 9

It was almost four o'clock. The Detectives decided to eat before going back to the office. Billy convinced Alfred to get Sushi. After ordering, they sat down in silence each trying to comprehend all that they had heard.

"Billy, what do you think about the wife? I'm almost ready to rule her out, but my gut tells me to wait. It's clear they have money, but I want to know more about their relationship."

"I agree. There is no perfect marriage. We're missing something."

"It's just too perfect, you know?"

"Yea, to hear people talk you would think they never had a fight, even newlyweds fight. Maybe not around the help, but they fight."

"I may be a country boy, but these people spend a lot of money at these churches, all except the Warren preacher. I need to check him out. He's the only one holding church in a shopping mall. Can you imagine being a member of that huge church only to wind up in some shopping mall? I'd want payback."

"Yea that was a long way from where he was. We need to check out the sisters, too."

"Man, they're something else. Since people join different churches then who knows what can happen. I mean, say you joined Jackson's church and found out the preacher you hate is speaking in a public place. That's a perfect time for revenge." Alfred deduced.

"Where I'm from, people stay at the same church for life."

"Ben should be able to tell us how long this poison took."

Alfred's cell phone rang. He walked outside to answer.

"Alfred, this is Lieutenant Radar. I just spoke with the wife. She wasn't happy, but she did agree to the exam. I promised her we would have her husband's body back within hours. The coroner should be there soon. Ben will start the examination as soon as the body arrives. I told him to expedite it. He'll call you when he's finished."

"Thanks, Lieutenant. We're heading back to the office. We've had some interesting conversations. We need to check some things out."

"Sorry for not calling the wife sooner."

"Thanks, boss, I know you have a lot on your plate."

"Let me know if you need anything." Alfred heard the dial tone which annoyed him. Radar never said goodbye. The man didn't have phone ethics.

Alfred went back into the restaurant and sat down. Billy was eating. Alfred gave him an update.

"You know I hate talking to that guy; he never says goodbye."

"He's rude to everyone, Al." They returned to the office. It was getting late.

Chapter 10

Returning to the office, they had a plan. Billy called Rev. Nelson to get some information on the Johnson sisters. He had a gut feeling and sometimes that resulted in finding a suspect. Alfred did a background check on Warren, Nelson, and Jackson. His focus was Pastor Warren. There was something he didn't like about him. His cell phone rang. This time, it was Evelyn. He walked in the hall then answered.

"Hey, baby, how are you?"

"I was just thinking about you."

"I've been busy."

"I hope I'm not bothering you; I just wanted to hear your voice."

"You never bother me. I love to hear your voice. It's going to be a late night. This case is complicated."

"I know you can't talk about it. Did you eat today?"

"Yes, you know how much I can't stand sushi." He chuckled.

"Yes, I know." She laughed.

"If it's not too late, I'll call you later," he said in a sexy voice.

"It's never too late." Alfred smiled. He was glad their relationship was progressing.

When he returned, Billy was on the phone talking to Rev. Nelson. He started pulling up background information when he heard Alfred.

"Man, the Johnson Sisters are well-known. The reverend was curious, so I told him it was part of our investigation. I don't think he believed me, but what the Hell. There's Tanisha, Marisha, and Elvita Johnson. They've been members for over five years and fought for Pastor Warren to stay. Instead of going with him, they stayed with Pastor Davenport. Nelson said, whenever they got a chance they stirred up messes."

"I told you they look like trouble."

"We can add them to our suspect list." Alfred printed background reports:

Pastor Warren was born in Macon, Georgia in 1943. He and his wife Eve have lived in San Jose for over 40 years. There's no criminal record.

Rev. Dr. Jerold Jackson is 70 years old. He's been married for over 37 years. There's no criminal record.

Rev. Myron Nelson is 51-years-old. He's been the Assistant Pastor at Mount Jordan for over 15 years. He was married now divorced. Nelson owns "Pet Health" a veterinarian store in San Mateo CA.

Alfred had a better idea who these ministers were. They all reported paying over ten thousand dollars for church tithes.

Warren appeared not to hold a grudge, but I don't believe that. The man's holding church in a shopping mall.

Billy interrupted. "OK, I checked out the Johnson Sisters. I love social media. The Sisters have a Facebook page. It seems they started a campaign to overthrow Davenport from being selected. Tanisha was upset.

Remember the one wearing the big crazy hat? Well, that was Tanisha. She's the oldest at 45 years old, married with three kids. The one with the red hair is Marisha. She's 44 years old, divorced with one kid and lives in Union City, CA.

Elvita Johnson, the one outside, is 41 years old, lives in Palo Alto, CA, no kids. Can you check them out?"

"Sure can." Alfred ran background checks.

"Looks like they all were born in Washington D.C. You're right about the oldest one, Tanisha. Neither one has a criminal record."

"Marisha Johnson is another story. She moved here in 1993. Divorced with one child and hasn't worked for ten years. No criminal record."

"Elvita Johnson has no kids. She moved to Fremont in 1996 from Atlanta, GA. Elvita works as a nurse. She was arrested two years ago for DUI. I guess she's the black sheep." They laughed.

"Man, you never know who you'll meet at the church."

The phone rang, Billy answered.

"Hello, Detective Parker."

"Billy, this is Radar. Listen I got a call from the president of the minister's union, Rev. Jerri Jones. He got a call from Rev. Nelson wanting to know why the police are involved in Davenport's death. It's just like I thought; this could blow up into something ugly. When you talked to him, what did you say?"

"We talked about Davenport. I think he's a prime suspect. He's next in line to take over the church. The church takes in more than a million dollars a year. Nelson is older and been at the church the longest." (Alfred handed him the background report) "He's divorced and a veterinarian. That to me makes him a suspect at least until we find out what the coroner has to say."

"Anyone else?"

"We still haven't ruled out the wife. They're worth millions. We found some members of the church that weren't happy when he became senior pastor. Some left and went to other churches. Some stayed even though they didn't like him. We need a membership list from Davenport's church and the other churches. I don't know if they'll give them up voluntary so we may need subpoenas but I'll let you know."

"Sounds like you're working on it. Listen, Ben called and said the body arrived. Check and see what he's got for you. I'll call this Jones preacher and get you the lists. I'll be in touch." Billy instantly heard the dial tone. Alfred could read his face and knew the conversation was over. Billy slammed the phone down. Alfred chuckled.

Alfred's phone rang. He looked at Billy shaking his head.

"Hello, this is Detective DeMarcus."

"Hello, Detective, this is Ben."

"Hey, Ben, what you got?"

"Listen, can you come over?"

"Sure, we'll be right there." He hung up. Billy heard the conversation and was already getting his jacket.

Chapter 11

They drove over to the coroner's office, parked, and took the elevator to the second floor. As soon as they exited the elevator, they could feel the temperature change.

"Man, I still can't get used to how cold it is on this floor."

Alfred led the way. Using his ID card he opened the steel door. It was cooler in the room. There was a line of five cold steel tables. Billy buttoned up his jacket. Dr. Ben Davis was standing over the table at the end of the room. He was speaking to the dictation machine attached to the two surgical lights glaring down at the body of a young naked African-American man. Walking toward him, they could see the body was in good physical condition. The face looked perfectly preserved.

"Hey, guys. You know you're lucky they hadn't embalmed this guy. Otherwise, there's no way we would get a clean sample that meant anything."

He handed his assistant a bottle filled with fluid he extracted from the victim's eyes. Billy turned his head.

"Doc, what can you tell about this guy? The last time we saw him, the EMT's said he had a heart attack. Then we get this report from the hospital saying, there was poison in his system." Ben explained.

"Well, guys, as you can see, he was in good physical condition. There are no abrasions or bruises except the ones from the EMT's made trying to revive him. See how the cuticles are black? That's a sign of poison in the blood, most of the time it doesn't show up until after death. If it were long term, I would have seen rings on the cuticles. I think it was a fast acting poison. The stomach contents show some green liquid which I sent to be analyzed. It doesn't look like he ate anything that day. See how the skin is somewhat yellowish? That residue is from the poison. Even though he died, the poison is still active. Check out his hair; it's falling out. If they wait too long before embalming him, he'll be bald. That, at least, eliminates some poisons."

"Why are his lips so dark?"

"Well, Billy, that's part of the residuals of the poison. How was he acting before he died?"

"Witnesses say he clutched his chest and fell on his face."

"Well, that explains his broken nose. He must have been in horrendous pain. This guy was gripping his hands so hard it left marks in his palms. I can see why they diagnosed a heart attack. Once I crack him open, I'll have a better idea what killed him.

Lieutenant Radar told me you needed the results tomorrow. That's not going to happen. Everybody is on overtime. Two of my people are on their way here. I asked Livermore labs to help. I understand this guy was a preacher?"

"Yea, we need to know how he died. So you say this was like a quick acting poison? Any idea what it could be?"

"I hate to speculate. Potassium cyanide could be the culprit. Initially, the hospital ruled it as arsenic, but I'm not so sure. I'm looking for needle marks. I'll call you when I'm finished."

"Thanks, doc."

Waiting for the results was going to slow this investigation down. They rode in silence, each absorbed in planning their next move. It was dark when they returned to the office. Billy broke the silence in the elevator.

"Listen, I was thinking, don't these churches have websites?"

"I don't know but check it out. I'm going to check out the preachers."

Having a plan felt rejuvenating. It was exciting and exhausting all at the same time. That's why they loved the job. The challenge was putting the pieces together.

Billy worked at the computer while Alfred gathered up all the paperwork and decided to review them piece by piece. It was hours before they took a break and decided to discuss their findings.

Billy found websites and started looking at the friends. Mount Jordan's website was intense. It showed meetings, events, and upcoming attractions. There was a picture of Rev. and Mrs. Davenport inviting the viewer to worship with them. He found the Johnson sisters and approximately 50 other members who expressed their disapproval of Rev. Davenport. Most of the time older people aren't on Facebook. Younger members were excited to be a part of the new vision for the church. There were over 3,000 friends on the site. It was evident; there was a serious division in the church.

The Morning Glory's website with Rev. Warren was a small one-page site. At first, members were happy, six months later there were complaints about worshipping in a shopping mall. Others said he was asking for too much money. Clearly, there was dissension in the ranks. They had 145 friends.

The James Tabernacle Baptist Church was the oldest website among the three. There were pictures of members, events, programs, and a link to the convention website. Rev. and Mrs. Jackson's invitation page showed all their accomplishments and past successes. There were over 1,000 friends on the church website. Billy decided it was too many to look up. He would have one of the office clerks go through the website and see if they can find any mention of Rev. Davenport.

In the meantime, Alfred couldn't find any income that equaled the amount of money Rev. Nelson showed on his income taxes. It didn't add up. He needed to dig deeper. He was surprised to learn veterinarians use a lot of chemicals including poisons.

They discussed their findings. Billy felt the finances of the Davenports were important. Alfred set his sights on Rev. Nelson. He was anxious to see what the toxicology report would say. They decided it was important to get subpoenas for the church memberships. That way, they could do a search of all the names to see if there was an overlay.

It had been hours since they took a break. Alfred's eyes felt strained. He walked out the door heading for the men's room. He didn't realize Billy had followed him. Neither one said a word. They washed their hands and exited. Billy went down the hall to get water while Alfred went toward the kitchen to make a pot of coffee. He could hear Billy coming down the hall yelling.

"Al, my brain is fried. If I don't get any sleep soon, I won't be good for the morning."

"I know what you mean. Listen, I've got a change of clothes in the car, I'll take a nap on the couch. Besides, I think I can go a little longer."

"Suit yourself; I'm going home. I'll get back here in a few."

"See you later." Billy left. Alfred could smell the coffee in the kitchen. He grabbed a cup and went back to the office. There wasn't a sound in the whole building. Alfred worked for a few hours and then decided to retreat to the locker room and sleep on the couch. It was too late to call Evelyn. Within a few minutes, he was asleep.

Chapter 12

That Sunday Evelyn worked from home. She hated to admit it, but she missed attending church. Having dated Alfred for almost two months, she still wasn't used to him not calling. She remembered the conversation she had with her brother. He told her the good and bad about dating a police officer. They disappear from their families and don't even come home. Every waking moment is used to solve a crime. She convinced herself she could handle the challenge. Today, she was feeling abandoned. Her head was telling her she couldn't handle this relationship, but her heart wasn't listening. She longed to hear his voice.

Evelyn kept busy. She wanted to help solve this murder so life could return to some normalcy, at least until there was another murder. She checked the website of Davenport grandfather's church.

It seems his grandfather, Will Davenport, was the organizer and Senior Pastor at Eden Hill Missionary Baptist Church in Charlotte, North Carolina. Even at twelve, he was a good looking young man. Sure enough, there was one article that indicated Gail had gotten in a little bit of trouble. There was no further mention of Gail. Apparently, money does talk.

The San Jose paper had several articles about his dad, Mr. Thurston. Some mentioned his son; Gail was going to Harvard. Other articles talked about him buying and selling properties. There was an article in the society section that pronounced the marriage of Gail Davenport to Yolanda Morris. For the most part, it seems Rev. Gail Davenport was a wonderful young man.

Evelyn prepared herself a nice dinner and decided to check Yolanda's parents on Facebook.

Yolanda's dad owned eight dry cleaners. Yolanda and her brother, Ray, attended private schools. Yolanda opened an art gallery in San Francisco a year ago. She was quoted saying, "I'm happy to be able to bring a diverse group of talents to the San Francisco Bay Area." Six months later she sold a sculpture for $1.4 million. She and her husband made a sizeable donation to the Oakland Art Museum.

Evelyn logged on the Harvard website and found two archived articles about both Gail and Yolanda. One mentioned Gail's achievements along with three other students. They acquired an apartment building, flipped it, and then sold it to the University for $10 million dollars. Another article praised Yolanda for her successfully helping local art dealers revive their business. It was impressive.

Evelyn was excited and wanted to share the news with Alfred, but he didn't call, and she became frustrated and eventually angry.

Evelyn turned her attention to travel agency business. Deborah called.

"Evelyn, this is Deborah. How was your day?" Evelyn didn't want to sound sad.

"It was productive. I worked some, and then rested."

"Glad to hear it. You seemed a little uptight yesterday. I was worried about you. I just called to remind you about the meeting tomorrow morning."

"Thanks, I know you're on top of everything. How was your day?"

"It was incredible. I went to church, had dinner with friends, came home, and rested. How's your Boo?" Evelyn knew who she meant.

"He's busy as usual."

"Well, don't feel bad. You know Alfred's thinking about you."

"I know," Evelyn said sadly.

"I'll see you tomorrow."

"O.K." They hung up.

Evelyn finished her task, took a shower, and went to bed.

Chapter 13

Alfred knew he probably wasn't going home that's why he packed a change of clothes in his car. Now he was lying on a small couch in the basement, trying to sleep. Having a lounge and shower area in the building was nice. Tonight, he focused on the case. He took being the lead detective seriously. His body, on the other hand, was thinking about Evelyn. Quickly he changed his focus back to the case. He slept for a few hours and woke up early Monday morning. It was 7:00 a.m. so Alfred called Evelyn.

"Hello, baby."

"Hi yourself, how are you?"

"Busy, sorry I didn't have a chance to call you yesterday. Things are crazy. I just wanted you to know I miss you."

"That's so sweet; I miss you too."

"I can't talk long, but I'll call you when I can."

"Alright, be careful."

"I will." He hung up.

After drinking coffee, she went upstairs showered and dressed. Evelyn decided to go into the office and do some paperwork. She found herself smiling just thinking about Alfred. Deborah greeted her at the door, and as soon as she saw her, she smiled.

"Girl, you look like you're floating on a cloud, you must be in love."

Evelyn didn't say a word she just smiled and walked back to her office. Even though she and Deborah had a special bond, some things were off limit, and her love life was one of them. Today, she just wanted to enjoy her feelings alone. Deborah turned and went back to her desk. She knew when not to push.

In a few minutes, Deborah knocked on the door and walked in with documents they needed to review. There were reservations to complete and calls to return. Today she didn't care how much work she had it was already a beautiful day.

Meanwhile, Alfred heard voices. He realized there were guys next door in the locker room. The clock showed it was 7:15 a.m. He got up, showered, changed, and walked into the locker room.

By the time he got to the second floor, he had a plan of action. As he walked through the office, he could feel his co-workers eyeing him. He was feeling the pressure. He opened the door to their office. Billy was already there.

"Hey, Al. Glad to see you."

"Hey, Billy, how long have you been here?"

"About an hour, I couldn't sleep."

"How about you?"

"Not so much. I was thinking about the victim. I believe that we're missing something. Here me out. This guy became the head pastor a year ago. If somebody hated him that much why wait this long to kill him? I think something happened recently. He's wealthy and working. Why? If I'm worth that much money, there's no way in Hell I would be working. He had to be getting a salary from the church. We need to find out his schedule with the airlines. Let's get a subpoena for United." Billy was intently listening, writing a list.

"I agree we need to look at that angle, but I don't want to abandon the idea that an old church member found an opportunity to kill him. I mean, we still don't know how fast the poison worked. Maybe it was given to him earlier in the day, or it could have at the meeting. I mean, didn't the preacher say some of the members were supplying food and drink? I hate we didn't suspect murder when we went that night. We could have collected everything he was drinking out of for evidence. Alfred silently sat back in his chair and contemplated Billy's theory.

Finally, he said, "I have to agree that's plausible."

"I say we get one of the assistance to go through the church websites, make a list of all the friends, merge the list and see if we have any duplicates. If we do that, it means those people attended more than one of these churches. We can go from there. Man, I love social media."

"That's a good idea." The phone rang.

"Alfred? It was Ben the coroner. "I have to tell you I've spent more time with this dead guy than with my wife this weekend. I released the body a couple of hours ago. My people and I have been here all night. What I can tell you is this: It was definite a poison that killed him. I'm still waiting for the forensic toxicology report to show exactly what kind. Whatever it was the guy never had a chance."

"His wife said he mixed some homemade drink every morning after he went running."

"Well Al, as I told you yesterday, he was in excellent condition. No health issues what so ever. The liver, kidneys, and heart shut down in minutes. That's why it appeared to be a heart attack. Tissue samples again confirmed it was poison. We even checked the body to see it there was a needle mark, but there were none. Whatever it was, he ingested it. I changed the cause of death from undetermined to homicide. I'll hold it for as long as I can. Expect a call from the wife. I called Lieutenant Radar and gave him a heads up."

"Thanks, Ben for the head's up. Call me when the report comes in."

"Sure will. Talk with you later. Bye." They hung up.

Billy looked intense and couldn't wait until he finished. "Was that Ben? What did he say?"

"Nothing, we didn't already know. It's was poison, but Ben still doesn't know what kind." Neither one of them said a word. Suddenly, the door opened. It was Lieutenant Radar. Alfred looked up, saw him, and sat back down in his chair.

"Hey, guys, what do we have?" Billy sat down and let Alfred talk.

"Ben just called and confirmed we have a homicide. He doesn't know what kind of poison it is, but its fast acting. He checked for puncture wounds but couldn't find so it must have been something he ate or drank. We're working on a couple of ideas. Ben's going to change the cause of death to homicide, and that's going to open this investigation up to the new reporters?"

"Yea, I've already received a call from an attorney representing the wife. The wife wants to know why the police are involved. I'll have a meeting with them to explain what's going on. Once the word gets out, I expect the mayor's going to have a prayer meeting in his office with every preacher in Oakland. What else?"

"We may need subpoenas to get the church registration for three churches, Rev. Jackson's church, Rev. Warren's church, and the victim's."

"Well, let me handle it. I'll call the preachers and see what happens, anything else?"

"Yes, since we'll be tracking down leads can we get some clerical help?"

"Tell you what, find somebody in clerical you can trust and I'll make them available just for you and swear them to secrecy." They all laughed

"Seriously, I don't want any leaks so pick wisely." "You got it, Lieutenant. Is that it?

"For now, that's it. We're still checking some other leads out. I'll let you know if we need anything else."

"Good, it sounds like you're making progress. Keep me up-to-date."

"I will." Lieutenant Radar turned and walked out the door.

Billy and Alfred glanced at each other in discontent, and then continued working. Billy called a supervisor in clerical to find someone trusts worthy to handle their needs.

Cadet Adam Walsh was assigned the task.

Chapter 14

When the funeral director called Yolanda Davenport Sunday night and told her the coroner wanted to examine her husband's body, she fell apart. Her maid Doris had to call her parents who immediately came to her aid. When told about the coroner, her father was enraged. He called Mark Benson, his attorney. Mark said it was unusual for the coroner to be involved with a death that was already verified by the hospital but that it does happen. Mr. Morris told him to find out what was going on and to make sure the funeral home kept their mouths shut. He then called Yolanda's doctor and had him provide medication to help her sleep.

Monday was a beautiful warm sunny day. Alisa, the housekeeper, arrived early. Knowing what had happened, she moved around the house as quietly as possible. If someone entered the room where she was cleaning, she'd quietly exited.

Doris cooked breakfast. Yolanda woke up, and for a second she imagined Gail was out jogging, and then her mind rushed back to reality. Gail was dead, and she was all alone. It was as if half her soul was gone. A wave of terror and hurt engulfed her whole body. Yolanda buried her head in the pillow and cried.

It was 9:00 a.m. and her father was downstairs in Gail's office. Knowing how grief-stricken his daughter was, he and his wife decided to stay with her for as long as they were needed. His son, Ray, was arriving later that evening. Mr. Morris called Yolanda's assistant Amy and asked her to come to the house and assist with the phones. He knew Amy could be trusted to keep conversations she heard confidential. She agreed. There were no words he could say to ease his daughter's pain. For him, Gail was a wonderful son-in-law and a great man. His attorney hadn't called him back to explain why the coroner needed to examine Gail's body, so he was concerned.

Helping his daughter get through this tragedy was the only thing on his mind. He made a list of things that needed to get done. The phone rang, and he answered it.

"Hello, is this the Davenport residence?"

"Yes, it is."

"My name is Lieutenant Radar with the Oakland Police Department. Who am I speaking to?"

"This is Troy Morris; Yolanda is my daughter."

"Mr. Morris, I'm so sorry for your family's loss. I received a call from Mrs. Davenport's attorney asking why the police are involved in your son-in-law's death." Mr. Morris wasn't going to tell him he contacted his lawyer.

"I'm glad you called; my daughter is upset enough losing her husband. Why did the coroner need to be involved?"

"That's why I called. Is there a right time for me to visit? I understand your daughter is very upset. I would like to explain to you face to face."

"We're going to the funeral home this morning. We should be back around one. Can you be here around 1:30 p.m.?"

"Thank you, I will see you at 1:30 p.m." Mr. Morris hung up the phone. Immediately he called his attorney and asked him to be present for the meeting. Mark agreed. He told his wife Vivian about the call. She, too, was concerned. As a loving mother, Vivian convinced her daughter to eat a small breakfast before they left. Yolanda's face looked sunken in, frail and weak. She tried to convince her parents she was all right but they knew better. Mr. Morris didn't know how Yolanda would react at the funeral so he called her doctor and asked him to meet them there. The doctor agreed. Amy arrived just as they were leaving. Mr. Morris made it very clear that whatever she heard in the house was to remain confidential. She agreed. Doris, the maid, was in charge while they were away. Flowers continued to arrive.

Yolanda cried the entire time she was gathering the suit for the funeral home. She dressed in an elegant black suit, a large black hat to hide her face with large dark shades. Before leaving for the funeral home, Yolanda's parents sat her down and told her about the call from Lieutenant Radar. She sat in silence perplexed as to why the police were involved in Gail's death. Her parents helplessly watched their daughter and wished they could make it all go away. Finally, she stood up and said it was time to leave.

Mr. Morris ordered a limousine to drive them around. They rode in silence. The funeral director met them outside the funeral home along with her doctor. The funeral director ushered them into one of the family rooms. Yolanda gave him the suit and other items. She wanted to see her husband, but the director strongly urged her to wait. The doctor agreed. With her parents help, she made the necessary arrangements. Yolanda was exhausted. They arrived back at the house around twelve o'clock. Yolanda felt it was time enough for her to take a nap. Mr. Morris kept the phone messages. Thirty were from ministers and church members. Other calls were from people in the community, but one was from a woman named Carolyn Johnson. Yolanda didn't recognize the name or phone number. Her dad left the stack of messages on the table near the house phone.

At precisely 1:30 p.m., the doorbell rang. It was Lieutenant Radar along with two uniformed police officers.

Doris ushered Lieutenant Radar into the library while the uniformed officers waited in the foyer. Yolanda asked her parents to accompany her. Lieutenant Radar introduced himself and apologized for the confusion. Just as he was sitting down the doorbell rang again. It was Attorney Mark Benson. The attorney sat in a chair facing the long leather couch. Yolanda looked frail in the large wing back chair.

"Gentlemen, I'd like to introduce my attorney, Mark Benson." They shook hands. Lieutenant Rader spoke first.

"Mrs. Davenport, I know you're wondering why the Oakland Police are involved in your husband's death. Circumstances surrounding his death are not what it seems. As you know, the hospital attributed your husband's death to a heart attack. Since he didn't have a heart condition, blood was drawn and sent to toxicology. The result came back. It found that there was poison in your husband's system." He paused. He could see the shock on the wife's face. "Mrs. Davenport there's no easy way to say this. Your husband didn't die of a heart attack. Someone poisoned him."

Yolanda's mother murmured, "OH MY GOD!" It took Yolanda a few minutes to comprehend what she heard. Yolanda let out a bloodcurdling scream, and then buried her face in her hands. The attorney ran to her aid while her father tried to comfort his wife who was also crying. Based on their reaction, this was not what anyone expected. Lieutenant Radar waited. He hated this part of the job.

The attorney spoke, but his voice sounded strained.

"Who poisoned him? When? How?" Yolanda continued crying, uncontrollably. Everyone was shocked.

"That's what we're investigating,"

"I don't understand who would poison my husband?"

Yolanda was shaking, and her voice was trembling

"Mrs. Davenport, is there anyone, anyone at all who wanted your husband dead?"

"No. Like I told the detectives yesterday, I can't think of anyone who would want to hurt Gail. Oh, God, I can't believe this." Lieutenant Radar turned to her father.

"Mr. Morris, do you know of anyone that wanted your son-in-law dead?"

"No, I don't know of anyone who would want my son-in-law dead." His voice was weak. Lieutenant continued.

"If any of you think of someone, I need you to call Detective DeMarcus. I believe you have his card. He's the lead detective on this case. I can't imagine your grief, but I have to ask you a question. Do you still have personal items of your husband that you received from the hospital?"

With a soft voice Yolanda replied, "Yes, I haven't the strength to go through them."

"I hate to ask but may I have them? I want the forensic team to exam them. It really will help." The room was quiet. Yolanda looked up at Mark. He nodded yes.

"Yes, if it will help you find who killed my husband. But please Lieutenant, when you have finished I want them back."

"I promise you we will find your husband's murderer. I'll personally return these items to you."

"Daddy, can you ask Doris to look in Gail's closet and bring the plastic bag?" Still shocked by the news, he opened the library door and called for Doris. Within a few minutes, she brought the plastic bag to him. After closing the door, he handed the bag to Lieutenant Radar.

"Is Mrs. Davenport in any danger?" Mark asked.

"I don't believe she is. Is the funeral still scheduled for Friday?"

"Yes."

"I will be attending along with the mayor. For now, we're trying to keep this investigation as quiet as possible, but it's going to be hard, especially with the press."

"I just can't believe this," She said with tears running down her face.

"Here is my card. If you need me for anything, please call." He handed the card to Mark. He said goodbye and exited the library closing the door behind him. He took a look around this elegant mansion and left. It had been a long time since he had to do a notification. He handed the plastic bag to the uniform officer and told him to take it to the forensic team. He drove back to his office.

Back in the library, Yolanda's parents were trying to comfort her when Mark interrupted.

"Yolanda, you have my deepest sympathy. Be prepared because the first person they suspect is the wife."

"WHAT? OH DEAR GOD! You know I would never harm Gail, you know that."

"I know it. I just need you to be aware that investigations start with the spouse first."

"So, that's why the Detectives were here. Is my daughter in any danger? I don't care what the police say. Yolanda wouldn't harm Gail, but I'm concerned for her safety," her dad asked,

"I wish I could answer that. Apparently, they are still trying to gather evidence."

"Mark, I want you to arrange for some security personnel around this house 24/7. Whenever my daughter leaves this house, I want two with her at all time. Have the alarm system changed and have motion sensor lights installed along the driveway. I also want security gates installed in the entrance, with an intercom system."

"Daddy, I don't know?"

"Listen, your mother and I are staying here for a while. I want to make sure we are all safe."

Suddenly he stopped talking and said with his eyes full of tears, "I can't believe this." He continued, "Let's ask Alisa and Amy if they can stay for the week? That way we'll have the phones covered. If the press gets involved having that gate will keep them out." He turned to Mark with a stern voice and said, "Make it happen, now!"

"I will." Yolanda stopped protesting. She was tired and left the room with her mother holding her hand. Her dad turned to Mark.

"Did I cover everything?" he asked.

"Yes, one thing I will tell you is if the newspaper's get this story they will make it a point to go to the church and ask the members questions."

"Oh God, I forgot about that. Rev. Nelson doesn't know. What's the best way to handle this?"

"Are meetings going to be held at the church this week?"

"I think so."

"Maybe you can ask him to cancel all meetings. He can say it's out of respect for Pastor Davenport. That way it will be difficult for the news media to talk to anyone before Friday. Is the quiet hour still Thursday night?"

"Yes, the funeral home will have the body at the host church by noon on Thursday. The doors of the church will remain closed until six p.m. The viewing of the body is from six until the family arrives."

"Good, that gives you a few days. You won't have to explain anything to Rev. Nelson."

"You get started. I want everything in place before the end of the day."

"All right Mr. Morris."

"You can stay here as long as you need to. I'll have Doris fix you something to eat." Mr. Morris turned and walked out of the library.

Chapter 15

At the police station, Alfred and Billy were going over different scenarios in the case. Billy felt he needed to know more about Yolanda before excluding her as a suspect. Alfred was ready to eliminate her. They decided to visit the art gallery where she worked.

It was eleven o'clock when they finally decided to leave the office. Billy stopped to get a sandwich while Alfred drove to San Francisco. The bay bridge traffic was horrendous. Once in the city, they maneuvered around to get to Union Square. They parked and walked toward the gallery. The gallery was a large two story building. The walls of the gallery were white. There were sculpture pieces in the middle of the floor and a variety of different art pieces on the wall. Some were African-American pieces others Asian with a mixture of glass and metal. A young African-American man walked toward them. With a soft voice, he asked,

"Gentlemen, may I help you?" Alfred walked toward him while Billy turned to look at the art.

"Hello, I'm Detective DeMarcus and that's my partner Detective Parker. May we speak to the manager?"

"My name is Victor Muse. I'm the manager, how can I help you?"

"We'd like to speak to you about Mrs. Davenport."

"I see. Please follow me." Alfred followed with Billy walking behind him. He led them to a back office. He walked inside and around the desk. It was a small room with art and sculptures on wall shelves. All that was on a desk was a laptop computer. Victor opened it as they began to talk.

"Detectives, please have a seat. We were heartbroken when Yolanda told us about Gail. To have a heart attack so young is just devastating. He was such a nice man."

"So you knew Mr. Davenport?"

"Yes, Rev. and Mrs. Davenport host black tie events here at the gallery. Pastor Davenport was a handsome man. When he'd come, sales hit the roof. I think some of the women purchased the art to impress him, but Rev. Davenport only had eyes for Yolanda. Sometimes he'd surprise her and take her to lunch. They were so in love."

"What kind of events are we talking about?"

"Well, sometimes Yolanda holds fundraising events for the artist. She lets other organizations use the gallery. It helps get an unknown artist noticed while at the same time paying the bills. A few times, the Reverend had a church fundraiser here. Yolanda is smart as well as beautiful. I can't imagine how she's going to survive. They were inseparable. I'm sorry, how can I help you?"

"How many people work here?"

"Well, there's Amy, Yolanda's assistant. Gerald is a sales person and me. Oh, and Andy he's the bookkeeper, that's all. We contract with a small moving company to help with the art pieces."

"Is there something wrong?" Alfred ignored the question.

"So you say Rev. and Mrs. Davenport got along well."

Looking puzzled, he said, "Yes. They still acted like newlyweds." Alfred quickly asked the next question.

"Did everyone get along with Rev. Davenport?"

"Yes, we're all Christians here, not like some jobs."

"Do you attend his church?"

"No, I don't, but Amy does."

"What's Amy's last name?"

"It's Washington, Amy Washington."

"Why are you asking all these questions? Should I call Yolanda?"

"Mrs. Davenport is aware we're here." Victor's face deflated.

"So, how successful is the gallery?" Billy asked.

"I'd say we're very successful. Mrs. Davenport makes it a point to promote new artists and gives them an opportunity to show their craft. I've been here since she opened and I love it. Our website has generated lots of new clients some of which are overseas. I'm just amazed at how she gets new customers. Last week, we had a representative from a Japanese buyer come in. He bought a great painting. It's awesome. I just hope she keeps the gallery open."

"Why would she close it?"

"I don't know; that's just what I was thinking. I hope I'm wrong." The detectives looked at each other in unison.

"Did you ever have a disgruntled customer?"

"Not really. The only time we had somebody who wasn't satisfied was when the piece was damaged when delivered, but Yolanda made it right."

"How?"

"Well, it was from one of our new artists who painted another one at cost. The buyer was satisfied. That's the kind of person she is. Is something wrong?"

"Is Amy here?"

"No, she called and said she would be at Yolanda's the rest of the week."

"Thank you for your time. If you think of anyone who may have had a disagreement with the Davenports, please give me a call." Alfred handed him his business card. They stood, shook hands and left. They took note of the price of some of the pieces.

Billy commented on how pricey the art was. Now they wanted to speak to Amy Washington.

"Al, all I can say is there's no way I could buy any of that art on my salary."

"I agree. I saw a painting selling for $8,000."

"Man, that's cheap. The sculpture that was in front cost $15,000. Can you believe that?"

"That explains why they have so much money. When I retire, I'm going to open a gallery." They both chuckled. On the way back to the office, they stopped at Subways. While standing in line Alfred's cell phone rang, it was Lieutenant Radar.

"Hello."

"Hello, Detective. I just left the Davenport house. They're devastated. I told them what happened. It wasn't pretty. I have the bag with the clothes the pastor wore. One of my officers took it to forensic. They'll call you when they're finished processing them."

"That's great. Those are the only items we have from that night. Thanks."

"Did she tell you anything that can help?"

"I don't think she had anything to do with his murder, but it's not for me to say. You guys need to tell me what you find. I warned her about the news media. Speaking of which, I've got to update the mayor. I'm heading for my office now, so if you guys need to call me, I'll be there. Anything you want to tell me?"

"No, having the clothes may help. We'll call you if we need to."

"That sounds good. Talk to you later." Alfred heard the click. He told Billy about the clothes.

"That's great. Why in the hell didn't we think of that? Maybe there'll be some residue from the poison."

When they returned to the office, there were two phone messages. There was a call from Mr. Harrison, the hotel manager at the convention center. The other call was from Pastor Nelson. Billy took the call from Mr. Harrison, the hotel manager. Alfred returned Pastor Nelson's call.

Billy asked for the names of the caterers and employees who serviced the room where Pastor Davenport waited. The manager told him the caterer was from the church. The hotel's staff only provided utensils, tablecloths, and silverware. The two employees assigned to that room were Miguel Cabrera and Michelle Carpenter. Billy wanted to speak to them if they were on duty that night. Billy agreed to be there in an hour.

Pastor Nelson said he called the funeral home to discuss the arrangements. Rev. Nelson wanted to know why Rev. Davenport's body went to the coroner's office. He was concerned. Alfred said it was the coroner's decision. He assured him the funeral could proceed as planned. Pastor Nelson told him the church was suspending all meetings for the rest of the week in honor of their pastor. Alfred asked for a copy of the church registration. Pastor Nelson agreed to have it emailed to him Tuesday morning. He said their church secretary didn't work on Mondays. Alfred thanked him and ended the call.

Chapter 16

While Billy was on the phone, Alfred decided to call Evelyn on his way to Starbuck's.

"Hello?"

"Hello sweetheart." Evelyn could feel her heart pounding.

"Hi, how are you?"

"Busy."

"What are you doing?"

"I'm signing papers. I found some interesting facts about your case."

Alfred was anxious to hear what she had to say.

"Really? Why don't I come over tonight and you can tell me everything. Besides, I want to see you. Hearing Evelyn's voice made his pulse race.

"Listen sweetheart, I got to go. I just needed to hear your voice. I'll see you later ok?"

"See you later. Take care." He quickly hung up. He looked around, placed his cell phone in his pants and discreetly adjusted himself. He walked back to the office and continued thinking about the case.

Billy was gone. He left a note saying he was following a lead at the hotel. Alfred knew Billy liked to follow his leads. That's why he appreciated being his partner; he wasn't afraid to go after any lead.

Alfred called forensics to check on the examination of Davenport's clothes. They promised to call him when they finished.

Because Pastor Nelson agreed to email the church registrations, he took a chance and called the other two churches. The secretaries refused to email anything until they spoke with their respective pastors. The secretaries said their pastors were off on Mondays. It was six-thirty. The phone rang. "Hello."

"Al, can you talk?" Billy sounded excited.

"Yeah, Billy what's up?"

"I went back to the hotel. I spoke to a guy named Miguel, who was on duty Wednesday night. He and Michelle were told to keep clean the room. The room was a staging area for speakers of the convention. Ministers went there before going into the main auditorium. Miguel said Rev. Davenport arrived around four that day. He was alone. According to him, Davenport had a garment bag and a black briefcase. He said Davenport never left the room.

The other employee Michelle saw him talking to some men who she said looked like ministers. Michelle didn't remember if he ordered food. She did say there was a caterer who identified herself as a church member. The woman left food, coffee, cakes, and water. Michelle told her the hotel policy didn't allow food to be brought in from outside the hotel but the woman just ignored her. As expected, they've already cleaned the room. I showed a picture of Davenport to the valet. He said Davenport gave him a $100 to keep his car safe.

The only thing the manager remembers was that a preacher died. He said nothing else happened. I have a copy of the security footage. Who knows? We may get lucky."

"What happened to his car? Is it still there?"

"No."

"Billy, that sounds good.

"Al, I need a break. I'll be in early tomorrow.

"Yea, I need a good night's sleep too. See you tomorrow."

Driving home Alfred left a message for Evelyn and told her he was going home.

She was disappointed.

He stopped and bought some frozen dinners. While dinner was cooking in the microwave, he sat down thinking about what Billy found. Before long, Alfred fell asleep. He woke up, reheated the meal and poured himself a glass of wine and called Evelyn.

"Hello."

"Hello, I got your message. This case must be challenging."

"Yea, I need some real sleep."

"Got a minute to talk?" Evelyn asked.

"Sure I was just thinking about this case. Billy went to the hotel and got a copy of the footage from the security camera. I hope we find something on it."

"Alfred, I found out a few things that might be of interest."

"At this point, anything will help."

She told him of her findings on the website. He took notes. He asked her is it a practice for ministers not to work on Mondays?

"Yes. Pastors often preach for two or three services on Sundays. Mondays they take off to get some rest. Most church secretaries work Monday thru Friday but that varies. They answer the phones and prepare the church bulletins."

"Good to know."

"Is there rules that govern who is in charge of the church if something happens to the pastor?"

"Most churches have an assistant pastor. They conduct church services if the pastor is out of town and help during church service acting as program movers. Most assistant ministers are older and have been at the church for a long time."

"Wow, I didn't know that. Am I right to say that churches have a meeting where members decide who will be the pastor?"

"Yes, that's correct, and some meetings are brutal." Alfred started laughing uncontrollably.

"Really?"

"No kidding." Evelyn chuckled.

"Would they kill if their guy didn't get elected?" Evelyn paused before answering.

"You know, I don't know but people these days are mean."

He pondered over the idea. "I can understand if the guy was just elected, but Davenport has been a pastor for almost a year. I just can't see it."

Evelyn asked, "Was he cheating around?

"So far I can't find any evidence of that. Billy and I went to his church yesterday. We overheard a conversation about the pastor. Maybe I'll dig a little deeper."

"Alfred, you never know what you'll find, so don't be surprised. I know if anybody can solve this case, you can."

Evelyn, "Did you say he was rich?" Where did he get his money? Was it family or outside?"

"No, he made a killing in the real estate market while in college. I'll check a little closer."

"Alfred if he was in the process of building another church that could also be a reason to kill him. Folks get crazy when it comes to the building fund. I'm just saying."

"Thanks Evelyn that's a good idea. How's your family?"

"Dad's doing well." They laughed.

"Alfred, give me a call if you need anything else."

"Thanks Evelyn, you can read me like a book."

Evelyn hung up.

Alfred read over his notes looking for clues. He felt the heaviness of sleep and went to bed.

Chapter 17

Alfred felt the warmth of the sun on his face. According to his watch, it was almost 7:00 a.m. He jumped out of bed, showered, dressed, gathered his briefcase and ran out the door. While getting coffee at Starbucks, he called Billy.

"Billy, are you at the office?"

"No, but I'll be there soon." Alfred continued.

"I'm going to run down a lead. I was thinking about Davenport's plan to build a new church. I want to check something out. I'll see you later."

"O.K. Al, I'm going to look at the security footage. I was too tired to look at it last night."

"That works for me." Alfred hung up.

Alfred drove to the San Mateo courthouse and parked.

He walked to the San Mateo County Clerk's Assessor's office. Evelyn gave him an idea. What if Davenport made some homeowner made and killed him for that. Alfred obtained a copy of the map showing property lines of Mount Jordan MBC. He drove by the church to check it out. Several houses would be affected by the church expansion. He parked in front of the church. A few minutes later, a woman exited the building. He was in an unmarked car, so she didn't recognize him as a police officer.

"Hello."

"Hello, can I help you?"

"I was just admiring your church."

"It is beautiful, isn't it? I'm Sister Davis, the secretary." She reached out to shake his hand.

"Nice to meet you, I understand you're building another church."

"Yes, we are. Well, I don't know if we still are. Our pastor passed away last week. He wanted to make our building larger by adding on to this one."

"I'm so sorry to hear he died."

"We're devastated. Pastor Davenport was a wonderful man. I don't know what we're going to do without him. If you live in the area, may I invite you to worship with us sometime?"

Alfred thanked her, got in the car, and drove away. He decided this case could be more complex than expected.

Al called Billy who told him Davenport's parents wanted to know why the police needed to talk to them. Al got the number. The phone rang.

"Hello."

"Hello, this is Detective Alfred DeMarcus from the Oakland Police Department. Is Mr. Thurston Davenport in?"

"Please hold."

"Hello, this is Thurston Davenport."

"Mr. Davenport, I'm investigation the death of your son. I'm in the area and would like to come by and speak with you."

"I'll be here."

"I'm on my way." They ended the call.

Alfred stopped at the gates of the Almaden Estates and was given a map to help him find the house. There was a gated driveway. He pushed the button and announced himself. The gates opened, and he drove up the driveway to a magnificent mansion. The house resembled an Italian villa. It was massive.

The front ornately decorated doors opened as he exited the car. A uniformed maid was waiting for him. "Hello Sir, please follow me."

"He was escorted into an expensive foyer with marble and gold fixtures, then lead into an enormous office. Sitting at a desk was a tall, light-skinned, older African-American man dressed in a very distinguish black suit. His hair was a mixed black and gray with a mustache that matched. Standing he was at least 6 foot tall. Alfred walked toward the table, shook hands and sat in the seat facing the desk. The man waited for the maid to exit the office before he spoke.

"Detective, may I offer you something to drink,"

"No, I'm fine.

"Why is the Oakland Police Department investigating the death of my son? He died of a heart attack."

Alfred was surprised he hadn't heard of the poisoning.

"Mr. Davenport, did your son have any enemies?"

"What does it matter if he had? He died of a heart attack."

"Please Mr. Davenport, answer the question." He paused for a minute as if he was thinking about the question.

"No, my son didn't have any enemies. He's a minister. I mean he was a minister." His demur changed, and Alfred could see the pain on his face.

"Has anyone every threatened him?"

"NO! I think he would have told."

"Was he having marital problems?"

"No, He and Yolanda had a great marriage. They were a loving couple. They still acted like newlyweds. Gail was looking forward to being a father someday." His voice was starting to tremble.

"Mr. Davenport, I'm sorry, but there is no way to make this easy. Initially, the hospital diagnosed your son's death as a heart attack, but the toxicology report shows he was poisoned." A look of horror gripped the senior man.

"WHAT! WHAT did you say?" He stood up so fast the chair behind him fell. His voice rose. "MY SON WAS MURDERED?" He began pacing. "OH MY GOD! OH MY GOD! This will kill his mother." Alfred picked up the chair and helped Mr. Davenport sit down.

"This is such a shock. It was bad enough to think Gail died of a heart attack but murdered. My wife has been under the doctor's care since he died. I don't know what this will do to her." He opened a drawer and retrieved a handkerchief. Finally, he looked Alfred in the eyes.

"Who killed my son?"

"Mr. Davenport, I don't know, but I am certainly going to find out." After staring at each other for a second, he stood up.

"I'm sorry for your loss."

The maid rushed in.

"Mr. Davenport, is everything alright?" She began assessing him.

"Nancy, I'm all right." She looked concerned. "I'm fine, thank you, please close the door." Reluctantly, she exited. He had regained his composure. Alfred continued, "I assure you, we have every resource available working on this case. Please call me if you or your wife thinks of anything that will help." He handed him a business card.

"Detective, if I think of anything I'll call you. My wife is coming home from the hospital this afternoon. I don't know how to tell her. I have to call her doctor. Is this going to be on the news? Dear God, is this going to be on the news?" He asked in a drained, soft voice.

"I'm afraid it may, but we're trying to be as decreed as possible. Your son was a respected pastor and reporters are always interested in a story."

"Does Yolanda know?"

"Yes, she was told yesterday."

"OH MY GOD! Is she in any danger? I haven't talked to her today. She must be out of her mind. I know Troy and Vivian are with her. Are we in any danger?"

"We don't believe so. Her father is taking all precautions necessary to keep her safe. Is there anyone else who lives with you and your wife?"

"No, but after what you just told me I'm going to get a security team to stay with us just in case. I hate reporters."

"So far, we've been able to keep them at bay, but I don't know for how long."

"Detectives, I…"

"I understand." Alfred held his hand out and shook his hand before walking out the door. As he approached the front door, he heard the steps of the maid behind him. She tried to smile as she closed the door.

Alfred had a clearer image of who Gail Davenport was. He was a respectable man who was loved. Alfred drove to the office.

Billy was glued to his laptop reviewing the security footage. He started with Monday through Wednesday. An Evidence Technician called and asked them to come to the lab.

At the lab, Joel, a technician, assigned to this case had Davenport's clothes laid out on a table.

"Hey, guys. I wanted you to see this before I put it in my report. First, let me say this suit is awesome. This guy was loaded." Joel was rubbing it between his fingers. "This suit costs more than my house note, but that's not why I called you; I found something interesting on the lapel. This guy died from cyanide poisoning." Billy shouted, "I knew it." Alfred just nodded his head.

"He never had a chance. This stuff works fast. That's why it appeared he had a heart attack. It was given to him maybe ten minutes before he died. I called Ben and gave him my findings." They thanked him and left.

Now they could put together a timeline. On the way back to the office Alfred asked, "Billy, any luck with the security footage?"

"Not so far,"

"Well, I went to the Assessor's office at Redwood City to check out an idea. Remember the wife said the pastor was planning on building a new church? I drove by the church to take a better look. That church is almost a block long. Davenport was going to build a larger church which means residents would probably have to sell their homes. I met the secretary. She was upset. I'm thinking what if the homeowners weren't happy about losing their homes and wanted revenge. It's just an idea, but I'm going to check them out."

"That's not a bad idea Al."

Chapter 18

Hours after Lieutenant Radar left, the Davenport's house was buzzing with activity. Attorney Mark Benson knew when Mr. Morris said to get something done, he meant immediately. Having been his attorney for over five years, he was on his cell phone minutes later. He had his secretary contact the security company. A private security company had two armed men dispatched to the house within hours. The alarm system was upgraded. Attorney Benson was able to get gates installed at the driveway entrance. He suggested they hire a phone service to answer all calls, but Yolanda insisted Amy should do it. Her mother took the limo to her house to get enough clothes for her and her dad. Mr. Morris remained with his daughter who was trying to comprehend what was happening. Amy would be staying at the house, so she went home to pack a bag for the rest of the week. Yolanda was so glad to have Amy. She would give her extra money for her help. Now Yolanda was sitting on the sofa in her bedroom trying to understand why Gail was murdered. Yolanda walked into her husband's closet and saw his briefcase on the floor. She realized only his clothes were given to the police. Yolanda clutched it close to her body and could smell the scent of Gail which made her cry. After a few minutes, she laid it on the island in the closet and opened it. Gail's Bible, papers, and other documents were still inside. His cell phone was hidden in a secret compartment. It was just too much to handle. She closed and locked it and left it on the island.

Ray was in Europe on a business trip when he received the news of his brother-in-law's death. He arrived at 6:30 p.m., from Paris and was shocked to see security guards at the house. Seeing her brother was comforting. They were close. Gail's parents called every day checking on her. Her mother-in-law had to be hospitalized when she heard of her son's death. Now the whole family was eating dinner. Amy still hadn't returned. Mr. Morris decided this was the time to tell his son what happened. After dinner, they gathered in the library.

Ray was shocked when told of the murder. Even after hearing it the second time, Mrs. Morris cried with Yolanda. Ray couldn't understand how this happened. He talked with Yolanda and Gail once a week. He talked to Gail on Monday, the day before he died. Gail was excited about expanding the church. The city manager had approved his plans.

"Yolanda, did Gail ever say he felt threatened by anyone?" Ray asked.

"Ray, Gail never said a word to me about anyone threatening him. If so, he kept it to himself. I just don't know why someone would want him dead?" Yolanda said.

"Dad, is Yolanda in danger? Is that why you have security guys? I hope the police find whoever did it. I loved Gail like a brother."

"Son, I don't know what's going on, but I'm not taking any chances. Someone killed Gail, so who knows what danger your sister's in. Until then, those men with guns will be here to protect us all." Ray continued.

"Dad, I understand, but I've got work to do. I won't be able to stay after the funeral. While I'm here, I'll keep my eyes open for any danger. Yolanda, Dad, and Mom will be with you, so I know you'll be safe. Is the memorial service still scheduled for Thursday night?

"Yes, Ray. I'm concerned about it. Yolanda insists on going. I hired personal security for that night and the funeral."

"I'll stay with you until Saturday. Dad is there a police escort for the two days?"

"I'm going to call the funeral director and make sure there is. I know they have employees they use but I may hire additional ones," his father replied.

"That sounds good, Dad."

"Son, please be careful. I don't want anything to happen to any of us."

"Do you think reporters will be there?"

"I don't know. I'll get Ben to speak for the family. I'm not planning on saying a word."

"I don't think any of us should say anything to anyone outside the family."

Ray hugged his sister. "Alright, baby girl. I know this is hard for you, but we're going to get through this."

"I'm tired everybody so I'm going to bed." Yolanda gave everyone a hug and went to her bedroom. Mrs. Morris followed. Ray and his dad remained in the library with the door closed.

"Dad, is Yolanda going to be ok?"

"You know baby girl is stronger than she looks. Your mom and I will be here to keep an eye on her."

"What's happening at the church?" He filled him in on all the happenings of the church.

"You know, it was hard for Gail to be mean to anyone?" Ray was thinking about how much he's going to miss his brother-in-law. Wiping his face, Ray stood up and gave his father a hug good night. These were proud men and even though the words weren't spoken, they were hurt.

Chapter 19

Tuesday morning Evelyn arrived in the office early and bought donuts for the staff. She had an appointment scheduled with her former pastor, Pastor Watson. She was looking forward to hearing an update on how the church was proceeding. Deborah greeted her, sat down and started talking about the day's activities.

"Evelyn, how are you today?"

"I'm good, how are you?"

"I got a call from a pastor in Sacramento who heard about our services and wanted to book travel for him and his wife. Before long, you may have to hire another assistant," she laughed

"God is good. I'll take all the business I can get."

"Pastor Watson called, and he'd like to meet around 1 o'clock. Is that good for you?"

Evelyn decided to get lunch before meeting with Pastor Watson. At 12:55 Evelyn heard the door open. Everyone was out to lunch, so she walked to the front and there stood Rev. Watson. Evelyn took a deep breath.

"Pastor Watson, it's so good to see you."

"Sister Jenkins, it's good to see you, too." They shook hands, and she escorted him to her office.

"Please, have a seat. May I offer you anything, water, coffee or soda?"

"No, Sister Jenkins, I just ate a hearty lunch. Thank you. It looks like business is doing well."

"Yes, it is. I have two employees now. The last time we spoke, I only had one, and that was Deborah. How have you been?"

"I'm doing just fine, and so is the church. We miss you. I've been praying the Lord will change your mind. Sister Watson asked me to tell you hello." He smiled.

"Thank you for your prayers, Pastor. If the Lord leads me back, I'll return. Please give Sister Watson my regards. Now, how can I help you?" He gave her his itinerary. After they had finished he stood up to leave.

"Pastor Watson, I just want to thank you for referring me to other ministers.

"It's my pleasure Sister Jenkins, you are a smart lady, and I trust you. I'm praying the Lord will keep expanding your business and if there's anything else I can do, please feel free to let me know.

"Pastor Watson, did you know the minister who died?"

"No. I spoke to Rev. Calloway who was there that night. He said it was such a shock."

They shook hands, and he left. Evelyn sat back in her chair. She still wasn't ready to return to Gabriel Church where she used to be a member.

Chapter 20

Back at the police station, the detectives were going over their leads. Alfred unrolled the parcel/block map of the street where Davenport's church was located. Two homes were in the path of the expansion. One belonged to 65-year-old Greg and Penny James. The other belonged to Virginia Magee, an 80-year-old widower. Neither one had a criminal record. Adam, the clerk that was working with the Detectives, said both homeowners were members of Davenport's church.

Alfred called them. Both owners said they were happy to sell to the church. Mr. James was retiring soon. He and his wife were moving to St. Louis, MO to be near their son. Mrs. Virginia Magee said she was moving to a senior living facility. Pastor Davenport offered her a good price.

Disappointed, he sat back in his chair thinking this was a dead end.

Billy was still working with Adam comparing membership lists.

"Al, what happened?"

"It seems the homeowners were glad to sell. Did we check the pastor who Davenport replaced that night?"

Billy, "what was his name?"

"It was Jordan Adams".

"Did we check him out?"

"No."

"I'll do it."

Alfred got on the laptop and did a background check on 47-year-old Rev. Jordan Adams, the pastor of Witness Now Church of Christ in San Mateo, CA. Nothing stood out. He had no criminal record. Alfred called the church.

"Hello, this is Pastor Adams."

"Pastor Adams, I'm Detective DeMarcus with the Oakland Police Department. I'm investigating an incident that occurred at the convention last Wednesday."

"Well, Detective DeMarcus, unfortunately, I can't help you. I didn't attend. I was supposed to preach, but my cold just didn't allow me to leave the house. Are you investigating the death of Pastor Davenport? They said he died of a heart attack."

"Well, that's why I need to speak to you. Can we meet tonight?"

Hesitantly, he agreed. "I guess so. What time?"

"What time is good for you, Pastor?" There was a long pause.

"How about six o'clock. My meeting doesn't start until seven that will give us time to talk."

"I'll be there." They hung up.

Alfred realized it was late. They stopped to get a snack. Alfred drove while Billy ate.

Traffic was heavy. Alfred was feeling anxious. The doors of the church were locked. They rang the doorbell, and an elderly lady appeared.

"Hello, I'm Sister Wade. Pastor Adams said you were coming. Please, come in." Smiling, she shook hands and asked them to follow her.

They followed her to the office of Pastor Jordan Adams. She opened the door, "Pastor, the police are here."

Standing before them was a stocky African-American man with a black suit and a white shirt. He was bald with a round face and a small mustache. His hands were strong.

"Thank you, Sister Wade." She turned and left.

"Hello, I'm Pastor Adams. Are you the detectives that called?"

"Yes, I'm Detective DeMarcus, and this is my partner Detective Parker. We're just gathering information regarding the death of Pastor Davenport."

"Like I told you on the phone, I don't know how I can help. I was ill last Wednesday and was unable to attend, so I called Pastor Jackson. I didn't know Rev. Davenport was my replacement until the next day and I didn't know him personally."

"So you've never met him?"

"Well, he was our guest speaker at the Church Anniversary Service, but I only met him briefly. Billy asked.

"Pastor Adams, can I say you have a beautiful church. How long has this church been established?"

"We've been here for twenty-six years this September."

"I can imagine you have some troublesome members." Pastor Adams eyebrows went up.

"You can say that. I learned early in my ministry that people are on different levels of Christianity. Billy smiled.

"Pastor Adams, may I just ask do you have any members with serious problems with your ministry?" Pastor Adams looked puzzled.

"I'm not sure what you mean?"

"I know not everyone acts like a Christian. Is there anyone in your congregation who you feel could do you any physical harm?"

"DO I HARM?" He shook his head no. "Gentlemen, every pastor knows his flock. Some members can be disruptive, but that's just the way it is. But to do physical harm, I just don't believe they would go to that extreme." Billy sat back in his chair and just looked at Pastor Adams. There was complete silence in the room.

"Are you here to tell me someone wants to hurt me?"

Alfred quickly spoke.

"No, no we're not here to tell you that. We're just concerned that maybe pastors have that fear."

"WHAT? WHAT ARE YOU SAYING?"

Alfred softened his tone to defuse the hysteria.

"We're not here to scare you; we're just trying to rule out everything." Pastor Jacobs was pondering over the question.

"I don't believe there is anyone who wants to harm me. Is that all?" He stood up. Realizing the meeting was over they stood up shook hands, gave him a business card and left. In the car, Billy said out loud exactly, what Alfred was thinking.

"He's lying."

"I know the reverend is hiding something. I want to find out what the hell it is."

Chapter 21

Traffic was heavy, so they had plenty of time to talk. Billy wanted a list of Adam's church members to compare with the list of members at Pastor Davenport's church. Alfred was trying to determine how he could get Pastor Jacob's to open up. Alfred would give him a day, then call and see if the pastor would share his concerns. In the meantime, he would check his lead with the homeowners. Something wasn't right. It was just too neat, families willing to sell their house to the church. Alfred decided to check with the children of the homeowners.

The Detective stopped at Starbuck's. It was dark when they returned to the office. Alfred was still excited. He was looking for that piece of the puzzle that would lead to solving this case. He could feel it in his bones; he just had to find it.

"Al, did you check the church's web page?"

"Yea, I didn't find anything, but I'll check again."

"Do you think your lady knows this guy?"

Alfred didn't respond. He was thinking about his conversation with Evelyn and didn't remember them talking about Pastor Adams. He would ask her, but he didn't want Billy to know.

"I don't want to involve her in my work." He lied. She was his secret weapon, and he wanted to protect her. He would ask her about Pastor Jordan Adams.

The phone rang.

"Hello, Lieutenant Radar."

"DeMarcus, what's happening? Are you any closer to solving this case?"

"We're checking some leads. So far we can't find out why he was killed."

"Listen, I've got the Captain, the Commissioner, and the Mayor breathing down my neck. Rev. Jones, the President of the minister's union, called and wanted a meeting with the Mayor tomorrow. The only way to calm them down is to tell them of the murder, and I don't want to do that. The mayor doesn't want to admit that especially since we've been keeping it a secret. They'll go ballistic. The last thing he wants is a press conference on the steps of City Hall. Don't you guys have any idea who killed the pastor?"

"I understand the urgency. But it's more complicated than we first thought. You know how it is? For now, we don't believe that the wife did it and there's no evidence she was in town. So we're gathering information from other sources trying to put this puzzle together. In fact, we just left Pastor Adams. He was the minister that

Davenport replaced. We think he's holding something back. We're taking your advice and handling it carefully."

"Well, maybe it's time to take off the kid gloves. This story is going to go viral sometime soon. The whole city's going to be up in arms when this gets out. You guys need to find out what the hell happened and why. Do it now!" That's when the phone went dead.

Alfred pulled the phone from his ear, "Damn him." Billy looked at him with a questionable look on his face. "What happened?"

"Radar hung up the phone in the middle of cursing me out."

"You can't let that guy get to you." He slapped him on his back, walked to his desk and sat down. Alfred smiled.

"Did YOU just say that?" Billy chuckled.

"See, doesn't that make you feel better? Now I'm the one consoling you." They laughed.

Alfred sat down at his desk. Billy began looking at the compiled list that Adam left for him.

After a few minutes, Billy broke the silence.

"Al, what's the name of that homeowner who was selling her house? Was it Magee?"

Alfred looked up and said, "Yea," he was thumbing through his notes to make sure. "Virginia Magee."

"Well guess who's a member of the Rev. Dr. Jackson's church, Anita Magee."

They stared at each other. Billy pulled a background check on Anita Magee.

She and her brother were born and raised in Redwood City, CA. Anita lives in Oakland. Charles Magee is 49 years old, married with two kids, and lives in Fremont, CA. Anita is still single. Anita has a criminal record for assault with a deadly weapon in 1965. She was also charged with a DUI."

Alfred called Radar and asked for a copy of her juvenile record then he called Anita.

"Hello, is this Anita Magee?"

"Yes, it is."

"Ms. Magee, my name is Detective DeMarcus I'm calling from the Oakland Police Department. I would like to speak with you" Sounding annoyed.

"About what?"

"Well, I can explain that when I see you. Are you available?"

"Listen, I've got a meeting at church, I don't have time."

"Well, I can meet you at church…"

She interrupted him.

"AT CHURCH! NO, I don't want you to meet me at church." Alfred could hear silence on the phone and knew she was thinking real hard about what she was going to say.

Sounding a lot more humble, "You can meet me here at my house. The address is…"

This time, Alfred interrupted her.

"I know." She gasped. He had her just where he wanted her, wondering what to expect.

"I'll be there within an hour." He hung up without saying another word. Sitting back, he smiled. He could feel the adrenaline rush. He loved knocking suspects off their game.

"Man, you've taken the gloves off. That's the Al I remember and love." He laughed.

"You know I'm a bad mama jama!" They both laughed harder.

They grabbed their jackets and headed out. Billy drove. Alfred compiled his questions and changed his attitude. The Bancroft complex wasn't in the best part of town. They parked in front of Building B. A group of young men were standing around talking. Seeing the detectives, they quickly disbursed. Alfred took the lead.

"Man, you look like a cop," Alfred snickered. He walked up the stairs toward apartment 208. Billy followed but kept an eye behind them. He knocked on the door, and it was quickly opened. In front of him was this short

African-American woman, who looked nothing like her mug shot. She looked older than 46, with a red wig.

"Ms. Anita Magee, my name is Detective DeMarcus, and this is my partner Detective Parker." She looked mesmerized. Then she looked behind him at Billy. Her shoulders dropped as she asked them to come in. The apartment was sparsely decorated in what looked like used furniture. The room had a musty odor. She offered them a seat on the sofa. Alfred sat down. Anita's focus was on Alfred. Billy walked around looking to see what might be of interest which made Anita nervous.

"Ms. Magee, we're conducting an investigation, and we need your help." Her body seemed to relax.

"What can I do to help?"

"Well, I understand your mother, Mrs. Virginia Magee, attends..."

She interrupted before he could finish.

"Yea, she goes to Mount Jordan Missionary Baptist Church where Gail Davenport was the pastor. Is this about my mother?"

"No. We understand your mother is willing to sell her house to help with the building fund."

"Yea, that's correct."

Standing behind her, Billy interjected, "Do you agree with her decision?"

Anita turned around and found him standing over her shoulder, looking at pictures on the wall.

"No, I don't agree, but it's her house. I can't do a thing about it. My mother and I have argued about it since she told me. I just gave up."

"Did you ever attend Mount Jordan?" Alfred asked. Anita turned back around to face him.

"Yes, I did until Davenport was elected." He noticed she didn't refer to him as pastor.

"So you didn't like him?"

"No, I think he just wanted the church. He didn't have a church before coming to ours. I like Pastor Warren better than him."

"So Pastor Warren is a better preacher?" Billy asked. Again, Anita turned around to answer.

"No, he's just an ordinary preacher. Davenport was all right, but I grew up with Pastor Warren all my life. I was comfortable with him. Then Davenport came and everything was turned upside down." The more she talked, the angrier she became. Alfred said,

"It sounds like you hated Pastor Davenport." Anita turned around to face Alfred.

"Yea, I hated him. He convinced my mother to sell her house to him. Can you believe that? When she told me, I went off. That's my house, I lived in that house all my life, and instead of giving it to me she wants to give it to him." She was standing up now, pacing. Billy interrupted.

"So she wasn't going to share the money with you and your brother?" She stopped in her tracks and realized they knew she had a brother. Anita took a deep breath and realized what she said. She sat down and changed her voice to almost a whisper. "Mom says she will divide the money between us," Alfred said,

"I'm sorry, what did you say?" Her voice changed to a normal volume.

"Mother said she's going to share the money with my brother and me."

"Do you mean the money wasn't important? You want the house instead?"

"I guess the money's alright, I can use it." She was looking around at her apartment as if she just realized what it looked like.

"Sounds to me like you could kill this guy if he hadn't died. Could you kill him?" Billy asked in a sharp voice. He was staring right in her face. Her body language didn't change; she was hardcore.

Sarcastically she said, "Well it's good he's dead." She put her hands on her hips. The silence in the room was deafening.

"Why are you so concerned about my mother selling her house?"

Ignoring her question, Alfred continued.

"So Anita, where were you last Wednesday? Were you at the convention?" Her head jerked around to face Alfred.

"Yea, I was there. I saw everything."

"What did you see?" He asked sternly.

"I saw him stand up to preach, then turn around, and fall on his face. That's when they carried him out. They said he died of a heart attack. That's what I saw. I don't miss him at all."

"So when did you talk to him?"

"Talk to him? I haven't spoken to him in almost a year." Billy asked.

"Are you sure you didn't go backstage and talk to him before he was to preach?"

"No, I didn't have anything to talk to him about."

"Well you could have asked him not to buy your mother's house, did you ever do that?"

"Yea, I told him. I didn't want him to buy my mother's house, but that was months ago."

With a very stern voice, Billy asked, "When, when did you tell him that? So you did talk to him last Wednesday?" Now she turned to face Billy.

"Yes! No! I saw him in the parking lot as he was driving in. He stopped and rolled his window down. I think he thought I was happy to see him. Well, I wasn't. I asked him not to buy my momma's house. He said he was sorry I wasn't happy and that he would give her a good price. That's all he said, then a car honked and he drove toward the lobby. That's the only time I saw him. Honestly."

Both detectives looked at her without saying a word. She was scared, and it was evident.

"So you were just standing outside when Pastor Davenport arrived?" Alfred asked with an authoritative tone.

"It wasn't planned. Hell, I didn't know he was coming. I have a witness; Sister Davis was with me. You can call her. She'll tell you I was with her all night," she stated with a cracking voice. "Ms. Magee, if you're lying, we'll be back." Anita went for her purse and gave Billy Ms. Davis phone number. It was obvious she was nervous, her hands were trembling. She took a deep swallow, and then sat back in the chair.

Billy went outside to make the call.

Now her voice was shaking.

"I'm not lying. I didn't see him again until he got up to preach. What's this all about?"

Alfred kept silent. He was staring at her. Within a few minutes, Billy returned and nodded to Alfred an affirmative. Alfred stood up and walked toward the door.

Anita stood and waited until the door was opened. She then walked toward them. Alfred changed his tone again.

"Thank you for your time. If you think of anything, give me a call." He handed her his business card. She shook hands, closed the door and locked it. They didn't speak until they reached the car. Anita fell on the sofa and started crying.

Billy spoke first, "Well, that went well." Alfred smiled and said, "Yes, yes it did." They both laughed. Alfred was disappointed. He hoped this might be the lead to this murder puzzle. It was going to be a late night. Alfred was too busy to call Evelyn.

Chapter 22

Evelyn left the office late. Alfred hadn't called so she knew he must be busy. If they were married, she would be furious. Instead, Evelyn was just disappointed. Surely he could have found a minute or two to call just to check to see how she was doing. That's why she was apprehensive about the relationship.

It was late when she got home. The answering machine was beeping. But it couldn't be Alfred because he calls on her cell phone. Pressing the button a woman's voice came on.

"Evelyn, this is Deborah. I left my cell phone at work. Listen, I called to tell you a friend said the police are investigating Pastor Davenport's death. I didn't know if you knew anything about it. Evelyn, do you think he was murdered? You know we are familiar with church folk murdering each other. My friend goes to his church. She said they canceled all the meetings for the week. I guess it's because the pastor died. She told me a lot of members at the church didn't want him as pastor. You know it's going to be messy when it's time to get a new pastor. Call me if you can. I'm going back to the office and get my phone. I can't live without that thing. Just think, murder. Got to go, call me."

Evelyn smiled thinking if she only knew. Deborah's comments sparked her curiosity. She'd been thinking about the case. Sometimes people don't share everything with each other but have no shame posting it on Facebook. Evelyn sat down at the dining room table, pulled out her laptop and went surfing on the web. She looked up Gail Davenport's Facebook page, but it hadn't been updated. She pulled up pages of his college friends. An hour later, she found an interesting comment which referenced an old girlfriend he had, but it wasn't Yolanda. A woman by the name of Carolyn Johnson posted a comment accusing Gail of being a liar and a cheat. She threatened to sue him.

Her current page showed pictures of her and a two-year-old son, Michael (no last name). Evelyn printed the picture. The boy looked a lot like Gail Davenport. Family members talked about how smart he was. An aunt said he was as smart as his father. Again, nobody mentions the father's name. None of Gail's friends commented about a child. Evelyn sat back in her chair in shock. Davenport had a love child.

Carolyn Johnson failed to graduate due to her pregnancy. She lived in Dallas, Texas so Evelyn couldn't understand if this information had anything to do with Gail's death.

She thought about it and decided it probably wasn't that important but if Alfred called she would tell him what she found.

Evelyn ate, showered, and went to bed. Now she knew what her brother meant when he warned her about having a relationship with a lawman.

Chapter 23

Wednesday morning, Carl Jefferson, the Mayor of Oakland, was in his office early.

He called the Chief of Police and asked for an update on the Davenport case. He was told the detectives were still interviewing witnesses. Carl was livid. As mayor, he knew this case was unusual, but he had to answer to the community. He didn't want to get blindsided by the news media. The president of the minister's union called demanding answers as to why the police were investigating Pastor Davenport's death. This was part of the job he disliked the most. He was determined to avoid any problems. All the press knew was that a prominent young minister died of a heart attack and he wanted to keep it that way. When they find out it was murder, all hell was going to break. He yelled at the top of his voice.

"Get me some results!" He slammed the phone down. He knew his message got across.

Twenty minutes later his secretary handed him a cup of coffee and phone messages. Reading through the messages, he saw the name, Ed Norton, a reporter. His stomach churned. The meeting at 10:00 a.m. was scheduled at the pastor's church. He told them that the death of Pastor Davenport was being investigated to make sure he died from natural causes. The Mayor asked them to keep the information confidential. He assured them his best detectives were on the case.

While they didn't believe the Mayor, they had nothing to suggest anything different. They gave the Mayor until that Sunday to determine what happened. He went back in his office.

The mayor called the Chief of Police again and made it a point to tell him to solve this case before the shit hit the fan. The Chief said they still didn't have a suspect. He called Lieutenant Radar who called Alfred asking for an update.

Alfred told them what he had. When he hung up, he looked at his partner who instantly said, "I know shit runs downhill, and we're at the bottom." They both smiled.

Chapter 24

Yolanda woke up dazed from the sleeping pills. The past days were the worst of her life. She missed hearing Gail's voice waking her up. Her parents and Amy were sleeping in bedrooms on the other side of the house. Security guards were circling the house; an iron gate blocked the driveway, and her husband was dead. It was overwhelming. Never could she imagine living without the love of her life. Tears rolled down her face and into the pillow.

Yolanda's mother softly knocked on the door. She was worried that her daughter had been taking too many sleeping pills. Yolanda remained quiet. Her mother walked in the room.

"Yolanda, sweetheart, are you awake?" Yolanda slowly turned over, sat up and leaned back on the headboard.

"Mom, I'm awake."

"Baby, I'm worried about you taking so many pills."

"I know you are, Mother. I'm not going to take any more. I was thinking about Gail. He would be so disappointed with me lying around having a pity party. I'm going to get myself together and be the woman he'd be proud of."

"That's so brave of you." As Yolanda got out of bed, her mother gave her a big hug.

"You know I love you. We're here to help you get through this." Her mom squeezed her nose.

"Baby, you need a shower." They both laughed.

"I love you, Mom. I thank God for you and Dad for all you do. Let me jump in the shower, and I'll be downstairs in a few minutes."

Her mother walked down the hall towards the elevator. Yolanda shut the door and showered. She dressed in a black business suit with matching heels, grabbed her briefcase, and walked downstairs for breakfast. The smell of bacon permeated the air. Seated at the table were her parents. Amy was sitting at the breakfast counter while Doris was serving. Everyone turned and looked at her with surprise. Her dad was the first to speak.

"Good morning, sweetheart, you look better. Where are you going?"

She'd placed her briefcase on the floor near the door and walked briskly in the room.

"Good morning." She thanked Amy for being there and gave her dad a hug before sitting down at the table.

"Mrs. Davenport, what would you like me to cook for you?"

"I'll just have toast and coffee, Doris."

"Are you sure? You know you haven't had a good meal for days."

"Thank you, but I'm just not hungry." Doris prepared the coffee and wheat toast. Amy dressed for work.

"Honey, it's too soon for you to be going to work."

"Dad, I need to get out this house. Gail wouldn't want me sitting around crying. I can hear him now, "Yolanda you are strong." Besides, I need to check in on the gallery. Amy, I appreciate you staying here, but you can go home. I called the phone service Mark suggested, and they will answer the house phones. Amy was feeling uncomfortable with people she didn't know. She was glad to leave. "You can meet me at the office once you've packed. Dad, I called the car service so they'll take me to and from work."

"Yolanda, are you sure?"

"Yes Dad, I need to do this." He insisted a security guard accompany her. He was still not convinced someone murdered Gail, but he wasn't taking any chances with his daughter. She agreed. She asked Amy about the messages.

"Yolanda, you've had over a hundred calls. I divided them up in a category. There is a stack of over forty calls from churches, pastors, and pastor wives. There are twenty-five calls from friends. Other calls were from members of the church and people out of town. There were calls for Mr. Davenport." Yolanda gasped. Amy stopped. The room was silent. Yolanda had forgotten that there were probably people who knew him that didn't know he was dead. After a few minutes, Amy reluctantly continued.

"Some were surprised he was deceased, and they left numbers for you to call. Finally, there are calls about the gallery." Amy handed a small box with the messages inside in order by category.

Yolanda put the gallery messages in her purse and left the box on the table. She called the office and told Victor she was coming in. He was surprised but happy.

When the car arrived the security guard sat in the front seat with Yolanda in the back. Ten minutes later, Amy loaded her car and said her goodbyes.

Amy couldn't understand why there was a need for security and she didn't ask. She learned a long time ago not to ask questions that didn't pertain to her. To show their appreciation, Mr. and Mrs. Morris gave her an envelope with $5,000. The new gates at the foot of the driveway opened, and she drove to work.

Yolanda felt strange riding in a car with an armed guard. She knew his name was Jessie. He was scary to look. Memories of the last time she was at the gallery flashed in her mind. That day, she was happy and feeling like she was on top of the world. Now her plans were to visit a funeral home to view her husband's body. Gail's parents, her parents, and her brother were going together. But no matter how many people would be around she would still feel alone.

Walking into the gallery was painful, but working would be good for her. Victor and the other staff members gave her a big hug and expressed their condolences. She decided not to introduce Jessie. He quietly sat in a chair near the front door. Her office was full of flowers. She thanked them, closed the door, sat down and wept. The smell of the flowers was just too much. She asked Victor to spread them around the gallery. In the office, she looked at the messages and began returning calls. Most of the clients had heard about her husband's death and offered their condolences. Yolanda quickly realized it was too much for her. When Amy arrived, she asked her to return calls. The inventory was in order. She canceled a visit to New York that was scheduled the following week. By noon, Yolanda was tired. Her energy level was low. She was ready to leave.

She called the car service and left instructions for the staff. Yolanda wasn't looking forward to the rest of the day. Her appointment at the funeral home was for 6:00 p.m. Before she realized it, tears were rolling down her face. At home, Yolanda pretended everything went well at work. She didn't tell her parents how painful it was. With the box of messages in hand, she retreated to her bedroom.

Yolanda recognized most of the people who called except several long distance calls from a Ms. Johnson in Texas. She called the number.

"Hello, this is Mrs. Davenport. I'm returning Ms. Johnson's call from last week." There was silence on the other end.

"Hello, I'm returning a call, my name is Mrs. Gail Davenport. "Whose number am I calling?" There was still no response.

Just as she was about to hang up, she heard a woman's voice.

"This is Carolyn Johnson. Can I speak to Gail?"

"Ms. Johnson, I'm Gail's wife. My husband passed away last week. May I ask how you know my husband?"

The woman sounded upset, "He's dead. How did he die?"

"He had a heart attack." She was curious as to who this woman was.

"How do you know my husband?"

"I knew him in college."

"You went to Harvard? I did too. I'm sorry, but I don't remember Gail mentioning your name."

"I knew him before he met you." That perked her interest. Yolanda could hear children playing in the background.

"Ms. Johnson, when was the last time you spoke with my husband?"

"We talk all the time. Gail spoke to me last Tuesday." Yolanda's eyes widened. Her body went tense. She felt a knot in her stomach.

"Was this involving a business transaction of some kind?"

"Yea, you could say that." The phone went dead. Yolanda stared at the phone. How rude, she thought. Who is this woman? She vowed to find out why Gail was talking to her. Yolanda has never heard about a Carolyn Johnson. Tears were gone. Now she was a wife on a mission. She started thinking maybe she needed to know what was in Gail's will.

Attorney Mark Benson was looking over some legal documents when he received the call. He tried to sound sympatric.

"Hello, Yolanda, how are you doing today?"

"Hello Mark, I'm doing much better. Listen, I was wondering about Gail's will. Do you have a copy of it?" There was complete silence on the phone. Finally, he responded.

"Yes, Yolanda, I have his will. Is there a problem?"

"Mark, I need you to find out about a woman named Carolyn Johnson who lives in Texas. And I want to see his will. Have you filed it yet?" He paused.

"Yes, yes I have. I'm still waiting for the probate court to grant approval."

"Can you bring a copy by the house?" Silence.

With a firmer voice, she said, "Mark, can you bring it by the house? TODAY!"

"You know Yolanda why don't you wait until everything dies down and you've had a chance to grieve. It may take a few weeks before they make a decision." Yolanda shouted.

"Mark, I don't know what the Hell you're talking about. I NEED TO SEE THAT WILL, TODAY. Make it happen!" Her voice was like a quiet rage. She ended the call without waiting for his response. Her gut told her something was wrong. She was angry and didn't know why. She was breathing fast, and her hands were shaking. Yolanda took a deep breath and sat down to compose herself.

Mark sat back in his chair knowing this was not going to be a good day.

Yolanda rushed downstairs and found her father in the library.

"Daddy, I just talked to some woman from Texas named Carolyn Johnson. Have you ever heard of her?"

"Yolanda what's wrong?" He could see she was upset.

"I need to know, who is Carolyn Johnson? This woman said she talked to Gail on Tuesday. I need to know why?"

She was shaking. He could see she was angry and put his arms on her shoulder.

"Honey, I've never heard of her. What did she say?"

"I got the impression she knows Gail very well. I called Mark and told him I need to see Gail's will."

"I don't think he can do that." Hearing the commotion, her mother came in the room.

"What's going on? Why are you so upset?" Her mother closed the door for privacy. Yolanda told them about the call. Now both parents were stunned.

"How did she sound?"

"She sounded like she knew something I didn't." The ladies sat down. Mr. Morris opened the door and called for Doris. He asked her to bring them water. There was complete silence in the room.

"I called Mark and told him to find out who she is. He's checking on it. And I want to know what's in Gail's will."

"Oh honey, you can't think anything bad. Don't get upset because it probably isn't anything strange. I'm sure Mark will clear this up."

"I hope so, Daddy. I can't take any more surprises."

Yolanda slowly walked upstairs to her bedroom. She went in Gail's closet. His briefcase was no longer on the island where she left it but was on the floor. Rage filled inside her. Her mind went racing. It was clear somebody looked through Gail's briefcase.

She stormed downstairs. Alisa, the housekeeper, said she hadn't been in Gail's closet. Doris also told her she hadn't been in his closet. That left her parents and Amy. Her parents denied they were in his closet, which left Amy.

Livid she called Amy at work and found that she'd left the office, and wasn't answering her cell phone. Yolanda was enraged. She opened the briefcase and found that papers were moved. Whoever looked inside didn't know about the secret compartment. The cell phone was still there. Sitting on the bed, she checked previous messages and was shocked. For four months there were flirtatious text messages from Amy. Gail responses were rebuffing her suggestions. He asked her to stop sending them. She apologized and asked him to please delete her previous messages. Yolanda knew Gail had a problem purging old data which is why the messages were still on his phone.

She was horrified. All this time she trusted Amy and now this. What else had she been doing? What other secrets did Gail keep from her? She laid on the bed her mind spinning, wondering how she missed the signs.

Chapter 25

The families decided to go to the funeral home together. The wake would be the following night at 7:00 p.m. The funeral would be on Friday at 11:00 a.m. Both services would be held at True Vine COGIC in San Mateo. Since Gail's death, the parents drew even closer. Mr. Davenport beefed up the security at his home. They had no idea what to do if reporters started asking questions. Mr. Morris asked Ray to be the spokesperson for the family. When her father-in-law called, Yolanda suggested they meet at her house so they could all ride together to the funeral home. Doris was to prepare a repast. When Gail's parents arrived, they decided to have a family meeting. It was the first time they'd been together since Gail's death. Gail's parents were shocked when Yolanda told them about Amy. Her dad called Amy a "disgusting whore" and demanded Yolanda get rid of her. Yolanda agreed. Then she told Gail's parents about her conversation with Carolyn Johnson.

"I remember her. Gail was dating her before he met you." Gail's mother stated. She turned to her husband.

"Thurston, you remember, she was the one who cheated on Gail. He was upset." She looked back at Yolanda.

"He broke it off. That was several months before he met you. I don't know why he was still talking to her."

They all thought it strange. It was hard to believe Gail was involved in anything suspicious. They ate in silence.

An hour later Mark was sitting in the library extremely nervous. The parents were sitting on the couch. Yolanda sat in one of the wing-back chairs. Mark was sitting at Gail's desk trying to look composed. Mr. Morris instructed him to get information on Amy and Carolyn Johnson. Mark was visibly nervous.

He started explaining why he couldn't discuss her husband's will. Yolanda wasn't pleased.

"Mark, I don't want the details I need to know if Gail had anyone in the will other than family." The look on Mark's face was priceless. Instantly, she knew there was something he was trying not to say.

"You don't have to tell me; it's obvious he did. Was it Carolyn Johnson?"

"Honestly, Yolanda I can't tell you, where did you get that name?"

"I talked to her." Mark was shocked.

"When I checked Gail's cell phone, they've been texting for over a year. Why was he still involved with her?"

Reluctantly he said, "I can't confirm or deny that she's in the will." Yolanda continued.

"Gail told me he had dated her before we met."

"Is that all he said?"

Mr. Morris interrupted, "Mark, I think you better tell us about this woman."

"All I know is that he dated her before he met you."

"Was he cheating on me?" Her voice was seething.

"I don't think so. Gail loved you."

"Then why didn't he tell me he was still in contact with this woman?" Tears were threatening to betray her eyes.

Mark paused.

"Mark, please tell us?"

"I didn't want to be the one to tell you." He paused.

"She had a child." Everybody gasped. Yolanda jumped up.

"What?"

"Gail didn't find out about it until he was engaged to you. Gail called me weeks before getting married. Ms. Johnson contacted him and told him he was a father. A paternity test confirmed that he was the father. He was scared you wouldn't marry him. As his attorney, I had to honor his request."

There was complete silence in the room.

The mothers started weeping. The fathers stood up and began pacing the floor trying to decide what to do. Yolanda sat motionless in shock.

Ray shouted, "Damn, so he was a liar."

Tears ran down her face. She felt betrayed. The mothers got up and smothered Yolanda with hugs trying to comfort her.

Mark sat back in the chair exhausted. He hated this. Mr. Morris was the first to speak.

"Are you telling me we have a grandchild by this woman?" Contempt was seeping from his words.

"Yes, Mr. Morris, Mr. Davenport, I'm afraid you do. Gail told me he was going to tell Yolanda. In fact, a few weeks ago he said he would." Mr. Morris continued.

"I just don't understand why he kept this a secret. Was he giving her money?" Attorney Benson replied.

"Yes, child support."

"For how long?" Yolanda yelled.

"It's been over a year. The only reason I'm telling you, this is because of the messages Yolanda received. I suspect Ms. Johnson called because she hasn't received this month's check."

"Would this woman be mad enough to kill Gail?" Gail's mother gasped. Mr. Davenport interrupted.

"I want you to check her out. I want to know everything about her up until yesterday. Hire whoever you need." Mr. Davenport was shouting. Mr. Morris nodded in agreement as Yolanda cried harder.

They all realized there was a grandchild out there that they've never met.

"Is this child a boy or girl?"

"Mr. Morris, it's a boy."

"So that's why you won't tell us about the will, Gail put him in the will, didn't he?"

"Mr. Davenport, I can't say."

"I think we all know he did. He turned to Yolanda.

"I'm sorry. I thought I knew my son but…this is so scandalous. He loved you. I just think because of the way he was raised he couldn't turn his back on this woman. As a minister, he couldn't forgive himself. His love for you was so deep. He would never want to hurt you. I believe that's why he didn't tell you."

She knew Gail's father was right. Gail loved her. He must have been so ashamed, but this is inexcusable. This, she could not forgive. Every time she mentioned having a baby he wanted to wait. How stupid she'd been. Of course, he didn't want a baby, he already had one. Yolanda screamed in disgust. Everyone stopped. The room went silent. They could feel her pain.

"Baby girl, I'm so sorry," Her father said compassionately.

Ignoring him, she ran out the room, upstairs and closed the bedroom door. Her mother sat down in disgust. She decided to leave her alone for a while. Ray poured himself a drink, wishing Gail was there so he could punch him out.

"Mark, I expect to hear from you soon."

"I will Mr. Davenport. I need to get back to the office." Mark quickly gathered up his briefcase, shook hands and left.

They all sat down in silence. Mrs. Davenport finally spoke in anger, "If this woman killed my son, I want her to pay. I don't care if she is the mother of my grandchild." They all agreed.

Doris heard all the commotion but stayed in the kitchen trying to remain invisible.

Yolanda ran to Gail's closet and yanked all of his clothes of the hanger and threw them in a pile on the floor. Her first instinct was to burn them. Instead, she yelled for Doris. Hearing the knock, Yolanda yanked the door open and told Doris take all the clothes out of the house saying she didn't care where they went.

Doris was shocked. Yolanda grabbed an arm full, rushed past her and through suits over the railing. She was raving mad. Reluctantly, Doris grabbed a handful of clothes and proceeded to take them downstairs.

Everyone ran out of the library just in time to see suits being thrown over the railing. Both mothers went upstairs to calm Yolanda down. The fathers began collecting the suits. Ray stood at the door watching the whole scene, drink in hand.

Chapter 26

Billy and Alfred worked late Tuesday night. They came in early Wednesday morning. Now that Lieutenant Radar gave them freedom to push the investigation to a different level they wanted to talk to Reverend Nelson and Warren again. Since Nelson was a veterinarian, he had access to chemicals. Warren could still be angry about leaving Davenport's church even though he said he wasn't.

Alfred checked the internet looking for the types of chemicals veterinarians use. One of the poisons used could be the murder weapon. That's why he still hadn't ruled out Nelson as a prime suspect. With Rev. Davenport dead, Rev. Nelson stood to gain the takeover of the church. Greed was certainly a motive for murder.

He turned his attention to Rev. Jordan Adams. While the secretary put him on hold, he decided to approach him more like a friend than a Detective.

"Hello, this is Pastor Adams."

"Pastor Adams this is Detective DeMarcus.

"Hello Detective, how can I help you?"

"Pastor, I know you receive information in confidence. I, too, have to obtain information the same way. When we spoke with you yesterday, I had the feeling you wanted to share something with us." He paused. "Pastor, I can assure you whatever you tell me it will remain confidential." There was a silence on the phone. He knew he was right.

"Detective DeMarcus, as a pastor sometimes we overhear conversations from our parishioners, but we try not to listen. I overheard a conversation that disturbed me and it was about Pastor Davenport. At the time, I didn't think it was anything. Members change churches all the time. I heard a member say she wished he was dead. I don't know if she meant it literally or not but in light of his death, I am concerned."

"Well Pastor, in my business, you have to understand I have to check it out. Of course, I won't share where I received the information. Your name won't be mentioned."

"Thank you. You can understand my concern."

"I can, but a man died. I need to find out if he died naturally. I believe the Bible says, 'Thou shalt not kill' so please know this if I determine that it meant nothing, I won't pursue it. I have to check it out." He waited.

"It was Sister Roxie Daniels. I recognized her voice. She was talking to another woman. She used to attend Rev. Davenport's church. She's been a member here for a little less than a year."

"May I ask when did you hear this conversation?"

"It was weeks ago at a Bible study meeting. Members forget that when they're talking in the hallway sometimes, their conversations are so loud that I can hear them. She said she heard that Rev. Warren got another church. I know it was a difficult transition to some members, sometimes that happens. Members don't like change."

Not wanting to scare him, Alfred took control of the conversation.

"Just let me check it out. It could be nothing. We don't have to talk about this again."

"That's fine with me."

"Thank you, Pastor. Keep praying for us."

"I will." They hung up.

Alfred told Billy what he learned. He ran a background check on Roxie Daniels.

"Al, it seems Roxie was a single, unmarried, 25-year-old, African-American woman. There was an arrest for a DUI and one count of possession with an illegal substance. The arrest picture showed angry, light-skinned, obese women with blond dreadlocks. She had a very distinctive mole on the left side of her lips. She's on the church roster of Mount Jordan a year before Pastor Davenport's tenure."

Alfred was anxious to talk to Roxie. He would wait until the evening to pay her a surprise visit. Besides, if police arrested everybody who wished someone dead, jail would be over crowded.

Billy wanted to question Pastor Warren again. He called, but there was no answer at the church, so he called Warren's cell number.

"Hello, Pastor Warren, this is Detective Parker, I spoke with you on Sunday."

"Hello, Detective, how may I help you?"

"Pastor Warren, I need to ask you a few more questions."

"Where were you last Wednesday?"

"Last Wednesday, I was in my office at the church."

"So you didn't attend the convention?"

"No, I'm not in that convention. I'm with a different convention."

"So you never went to the convention at all?"

"No."

"Did you know Rev. Davenport was going to preach?"

"I don't care about that convention so no I didn't know he was going to preach. I only found out about it when one of my members called and told me he died."

"Was your secretary at the church with you?" Billy continued.

"Yes, we're setting up a men's retreat. We were contacting hotels to schedule a date."

"You won't mind if I confirm this with your secretary?"

"No, I don't mind. I only go to my office once a week. We don't have the funds to hire a full-time secretary. Call her at this number." He gave Billy the number.

"Listen, Detective, what is this about?"

"We're just doing a follow-up. Thank you." Quickly he hung up not wanting to go into detail.

Billy called the secretary's number. She confirmed the reverend's story. His name was put on the back burner but not eliminated from the suspect list.

Elvita Johnson, one of the sisters he overheard bad-mouthing the pastor, was next on his list. As a nurse aid, she has access to drugs which makes her a suspect. Looking for additional information, he asked Alfred to look at her Facebook page.

Posted were pictures, invitations, and post. Alfred found an interesting conversation between sister Tanisha and Elvita about attending a musical at the convention. Elvita posted that Pastor Davenport was leaving. Alfred made a notation, to ask her what she meant by that during questioning.

Alfred knew this case was complicated but some of these church people are malicious. With the mayor breathing down his back Alfred knew they needed a break in this case.

Chapter 27

Evelyn was up early Wednesday morning. She still hadn't heard from Alfred. It wasn't as if Evelyn needed him to call; she was hoping he would. She was feeling guilty for withholding the information she found. Evelyn believed Pastor Davenport was poisoned at the convention center. It could have been in the guest room where the ministers stayed.

She looked through the convention program to see if anyone was assigned to assist the ministers. Sure enough, the Hospitality Committee of James Tabernacle Baptist Church was responsible for assisting the guest ministers. It's normal for the host church to help in this type of settings. Could a member of this committee be responsible? She thought to herself. Evelyn was curious. She checked the church website to see who was on the committee.

Listed on the church website were all members of the committees. There were five ladies listed on the Hospitality Committee. Sisters Mary Jo Anderson is the chair lady. Her assistances are Helen Watts, Joann Kennedy, Avis Daniels, and Patricia Cooley.

Evelyn pulled up their Facebook pages to see if there was any connection with Jordan Missionary Baptist

Church of Redwood City. Of the five, Avis Daniels was the only one who stood out.

The Daniels families were members of Rev. Davenport's church from the beginning. Evelyn wondered why Avis left. Of course, it could be nothing but it was a thought. To poison, someone meant it was personal.

Evelyn researched the family on Facebook. Sure enough, there were earlier posts by a cousin Ben Daniels wishing Avis happy birthday. It was a light bulb moment. They were relatives. Could that be a motive? Providing food and drinks would be a perfect opportunity to poison him. She sat back in the chair, took a deep breath and wondered what if she was right?

Chapter 28

After going ballistic, Yolanda finally calmed down. She agreed to go to the funeral home. The Davenports were wondering why Gail didn't tell them about a grandson. And the Morris' were scared that Gail was not the man they thought. Everyone was concerned about Yolanda.

Ray wasn't helping the situation by getting tipsy. In the limousine, everyone except Ray was trying to comfort Yolanda. They asked her to remain calm and wait until there was real proof that Gail had betrayed her. She agreed not to make a scene, but in her mind she had doubts. Yolanda had on a large black hat with a black veil to cover her face. Secretly, Ray wasn't surprised to hear Gail had secrets. What he hated was that it hurt his sister. Now he wasn't sorry that he was dead.

The funeral director met them at the entrance. He offered his condolences and ushered them into the chapel where in front was the casket of the Rev. Gail Davenport. The smell of the flowers was overwhelming. The Director explained that he had taken care to present the pastor in the best likeliness possible.

Slowly they walked toward the casket. Mrs. Davenport was overwhelmed. Having to bury her only son was just too much. Mr. Davenport strong-armed his wife to the nearest pew before she completely collapsed. Mr. Morris was holding his wife and daughter. Ray held his sister's hand. Mr. Morris stopped and helped his wife sit down in the front row. Yolanda continued toward the casket. Removing the veil she stood staring at the body of her husband. Her heart melted. Gail was the man she loved. He supported her and cared for her. Her body was shaking as tears ran down her face. She wanted him back. Ray held her close as she cried. Her dad joined them as he hugged her and whispered, "You're going to get through this." Her body crumpled to the floor. Ray picked her up and placed her on the pew. Her whaling broke his heart. All he could do was hold her close and wish he could fix things. After an hour they were composed enough to leave. It was silent on the ride home. Gail's parents left for home. Mrs. Davenport was exhausted. Her husband said he would call the doctor to tend to her when they got home.

The Morris' were also exhausted. They went to their bedroom to rest. Ray poured himself a drink and lay out on the patio rehashing the day's events. Yolanda retreated to her bedroom. Doris realized they were in no mood to eat. Leaving the food in the warmer, she went to her room. She, too, was missing the pastor and was feeling remorse from all that had happened. The next couple of days would be hard.

Chapter 29

Billy and Alfred were frustrated. At that very moment, Alfred's phone rang. It was Evelyn. Alfred immediately apologized for not calling. As soon as she heard his voice, her heart melted. His soft voice in her ear sent shivers down her spine. Embarrassed at her reaction, she lied and said she understood. Evelyn shared with him her findings. Alfred was stunned. He promised to call her later.

From the look on Alfred's face, Billy knew something significant happened. Alfred told him about the love child. Billy didn't ask where the information came from he was just glad to have it. He went to the computer to look up Carolyn Johnson. She's a single mother with a male child of a prominent pastor married to a very wealthy woman; that certainly was a motive for murder. Billy said,

"Carolyn lives in Dallas Texas and works in a bookstore. The tax returns showed she earns $27,000 a year. The house she lives in is worth $450,000 well more than she could afford. So the question is, what's her other source of income?"

Billy revisited Gail's finances, and sure enough, Gail was paying the mortgage. The property was co-owned with Melvin Schwarz, a classmate. They had purchased the house before Gail married Yolanda. He hid the mortgage payments as property expenses. Meanwhile, Alfred was looking up information on Avis Daniels.

The Daniel family was members of the church for over ten years. When Rev. Davenport was nominated to be the new pastor, they led the fight against his appointment. So when Davenport became the Senior Pastor, he removed them from key positions and replaced them with members who supported him. They left and joined different churches. Since Avis Daniels was a member of the Hospitality Committee at the convention, she too became a suspect.

Billy stood at the chalkboard and created a list of suspects and evidence. On the list were the preachers, the sisters, and now, Carolyn Johnson and Avis Daniels. Billy had an epiphany. He still felt Yolanda had reason to kill her husband. As far as Billy was concerned, they hadn't thoroughly eliminated her as a suspect.

"Al, what do think about the wife?" With a questionable look on his face, Alfred realized they hadn't approached the case in the usual manner. The spouse is always the prime suspect until proven innocent. Because the victim was a minister, they'd approached the murder differently.

"You know, we need to go there?"

Alfred pulled up the financial data on the gallery. The gallery profited over two million dollars last year which for them ruled out a motive for money. They both had life insurance policies worth over a million dollars. But they hadn't checked for infidelity nor ruled any other motive.

"What about the love child?" Billy pulled up birth information.

"I can't see any woman, no matter how wealthy, accepting the fact that her husband was paying money for a love child. Hell, my mother would kill my dad if she found out he had a love child stashed away."

"Billy, we…"

"I know I'll get my coat."

Rush hour traffic was heavy, but 45 minutes later they were blocks from Yolanda's residence. Approaching, they could see the new gate leading up the driveway. Billy rang the intercom. The housekeeper answered. The gates opened, and they drove inside. Unlike the last time, there were men in black suits who looked armed walking the premises. The detectives took note of the new surroundings. It was getting late, so the lights outside were coming on.

Just as they approached the doors, Doris opened it.

"Hello, Detectives"

"Hello, we need to speak to Mrs. Davenport." She escorted them into the library. Because they came unannounced, she was afraid of Yolanda's reaction. A few minutes later Yolanda appeared with her parents. She'd been crying.

"Hello, Detectives, have you found who killed my husband?"

"Hello, Mrs. Davenport, Mr. and Mrs. Morris. We're still investigating this case."

They all sat down.

"Mrs. Davenport, why didn't you tell us your husband was paying child support?" They watched her reaction. The pain on her face told the real story. She knew. They all knew.

"Is there some reason why you didn't tell us when we talked to you earlier?"

"Yes, because we just found out about it, today," she said defiantly.

"What do you mean, 'we'?"

"I mean me, my parents and Mr. and Mrs. Davenport. Carolyn Johnson called and asked to speak to my husband. She wouldn't tell me who she was so I had my attorney find out. Mr. Benson explained to us about the child. I checked Gail's cell phone, and sure enough, he's been calling and texting her." Alfred stood up stunned.

"Your husband's parents didn't know about the child?"

"No, they were as shocked as we are." Billy was walking around the room looking for pictures.

"Why didn't you tell us you had your husband's cell phone? "

"I didn't think it was important."

"That phone may help us solve this case." Angrily he asked, "What else do you have?"

"When Deacon Hamilton and his wife drove Gail's car home Wednesday night I was out of my mind. His briefcase was in it, but there's nothing of interest just papers he used for his sermon." Alfred raised his voice.

"This is the first time you mention a Deacon Hamilton. How did he get the car?"

"He was at the hotel the night Gail died. Whenever Gail preached, he always liked to have a deacon accompany him. Deacon Hamilton couldn't go with him, so they met at the hotel."

"What is his whole name?"

"John Hamilton. His wife is Beth Hamilton. They were so concerned about me. Deacon Hamilton didn't want me to worry about anything. I didn't think it was important."

"Let us be the judge of that. We need the car and everything that was in it. It may not seem important to you, but it certainly may shed light on how or why your husband died." Mr. and Mrs. Morris looked shocked and urged Yolanda to give them what they asked. She left the room and returned with the car keys, the password to the cell phone and everything that was in the briefcase.

"So, how do you feel knowing your husband was supporting a child?" Billy asked. Angrily she replied.

"I'm mad as Hell. I thought we shared everything and to find out he had a child is unforgivable." She looked at her parents. She was embarrassed and sat down.

"Mr. Morris, did you know about this child?" Mr. Morris looked puzzled. "No, we just found out about this today." Alfred stared at him observing his facial expression. He turned to the mother "So your son-in-law didn't tell you about this woman or your grandchild?"

"NO!"

"And you've never met her?"

"I think Gail talked about her when he was in college but I never met her. We knew he dated other girls, but it wasn't serious."

Looking at Yolanda, "And you've never met Carolyn Johnson?"

"No, he dated her before we met, but I got the feeling it wasn't serious." She told them everything the attorney reported to her. The detectives didn't believe her.

"Who's Melvin Schwarz?"

"Melvin. He was a classmate of Gail. They graduated together."

"When did you speak with him last?"

"Melvin? He called and left a message of condolences. I haven't called him back." Billy changed subjects, diverting her attention.

"I see you have security guards."

"I hired them to stay until you tell me my daughter's life is not in danger. I also had the security gate installed to make sure reporters don't invade the property. Is that against the law?"

"No, it's not Mr. Morris. We'll check to make sure they have permits to carry firearms before we go."

They stood up, gathering the briefcase and phone.

Starring at Yolanda Alfred said, "If you find anything else or get any strange phone calls, contact me immediately."

He gave her another business card. She gave him the list of the people who called and asked him to return it when they found the killer. Alfred agreed. They turned and left. Permits for the security guards were in order.

In the car Alfred called dispatch and made arrangements for the car to be picked up. Billy called the crime lab and told them about the items he was bringing in. He asked that they process the items as soon as possible.

While the Detectives drove to Davenport's parent's house, they discussed the case. They both felt this could be a turning point in solving this crime. As they approached the house, they could see that the parents also had security guards.

Mr. Davenport was shocked to hear the detectives were at his door. Visiting unannounced had a tendency to scare people and loosen their tongues. The parents were upset to learn their son had a child. They told the same story as Yolanda. Mrs. Davenport vaguely remembered Gail dating a Carolyn but didn't know her last name. They didn't have any other information to offer. On the way back to the office, Billy was so mad he wanted everyone to take a lie detector test. For the moment, Alfred was reluctant.

They took the items obtained from Yolanda to the crime lab. At the office, Alfred called Lieutenant Rader and gave him an update. He requested a subpoena for the cell phone company to get a dump of all the calls on Gail's phone. Billy looked through the briefcase. He even found the secret compartment. There were notes for a sermon, financial documents for property in Dallas, Texas and other miscellaneous items.

They felt the adrenaline rush. This lead was promising. Billy did a background check on Melvin Schwarz. As expected he purchased property with Gail while they were sophomores in college. They still owned two houses and an apartment building in Texas. Melvin's earnings for the past year were over two million dollars. Along with the property in Dallas, he was the sole owner of property in Southern California where he resided. Billy followed his intuition and called him.

After a few rings, Melvin answered.

"Hello, is this Melvin Schwarz?"

"Yes."

"My name is Detective Billy Parker. I'm with the Oakland police. I'm conducting an investigation into the death of Rev. Gail Davenport."

"What do you mean? I thought Gail died of a heart attack."

"We investigate the death of high-profile members of the community."

"How can I help you Detective Parker?"

"Are you attending the services tomorrow?"

"Yes, I am."

"Well, before you leave town can I ask you to stop by our office to answer a few questions?"

"I can do that. I'm staying in town for few days."

Billy gave him the address and set up an appointment for eleven o'clock the next day. He walked to the chalkboard and added Melvin's name to the suspect list.

Alfred was too busy to notice. He was thumbing through Gail's phone. It was jammed pack with information and messages. The text messages from Amy made her a suspect. Alfred concentrated his attention on text messages from Carolyn. The most recent one was two days before Gail died. It was an ongoing conversation discussing money. Carolyn threatened to tell Yolanda about the child. Gail was trying to convince her to keep quiet. On the day of his death, Gail texted Deacon Hamilton and asked him to meet at the hotel. Alfred felt a knot in his stomach.

He did a background check on the Hamilton's. They were married for twenty years and relocated from Houston, Texas six months earlier. Neither one had a criminal record. Mr. Hamilton works in construction, and his wife is a homemaker. They lived in Palo Alto, CA. Nothing stood out. Alfred couldn't understand how they missed this guy. He's on the church roll along with eight other deacons. Alfred looked at his notes, and there was no mention of Hamilton that Wednesday night or since. He called the Palo Alto Police and asked if they had anything on John Hamilton. Their records were clean. He called the Houston Police Department, and they had nothing on the Hamilton's.

Alfred and Billy were exhausted and decided to call it a night. Tomorrow was going to be brutal. At home, Alfred called Evelyn. They talked for over an hour. He went to bed. He wasn't feeling romantic at all. Evelyn told him it wasn't unusual for a deacon to accompany his pastors.

Chapter 30

Alfred couldn't sleep. Around 3:00 a.m. he brewed a pot of coffee and studied his notes. Billy texted him and asked if he was awake. Alfred smiled. They talked for an hour and agreed to take the Johnson sisters and Pastor Warren off the suspect list.

Driving to work he called Evelyn.

"Alfred, you sound tired. Are you getting any sleep?" He lied and said he was, but in truth, this case was complex. He promised to call her later that day.

The service for Rev. Gail Davenport was today, and Alfred didn't feel any closer to solving this murder. He and Billy were in the office by 7:00 a.m. Billy called Ben at the coroner's office who confirmed the poison was so powerful that it shut down Davenport's kidneys and liver within minutes. According to the coroner, Gail's body went into shock producing the excessive sweating and heartbeat. By then, it was too late to prevent his death. His heart simply stopped.

"Billy, it was potassium cyanide. It dissolves in water. I already called Lieutenant Radar and the Mayor."

Billy was stunned. He told Alfred. The look on Alfred's face was beyond words. Poisoning is personal. Rev. Nelson didn't have the opportunity, so the Detectives eliminated him.

Minutes later, Lieutenant Radar called asking Alfred for an update. Radar wasn't pleased to hear they were eliminating suspects. He reminded Alfred of the service that night and urged him to solve the case. Alfred held his temper. He called Rev. Nelson.

Rev. Nelson gave him the schedule for the services. He said the funeral home would take the body to True Vine Church of God in Christ in San Mateo, CA. It will remain there until the funeral the following day. After the funeral, they would drive to the cemetery for burial. Tonight, service begins at 7 p.m. According to Rev. Nelson, the casket will remain open until the family arrives. Then it's closed. Once everyone is seated the family comes in surrounded by pastors and dignitaries." He continued,

"Sister Davenport asked that no one approach her. When service is over, the family leaves. The congregation remains seated." Alfred asked, "Is that normal?"

"Yes. Families like to keep their distance. People want to shake their hands, and it can be overwhelming. Sister Davenport is very fragile, so we want to respect her wishes." Rev. Nelson, "What happens tomorrow?"

"Well Detective, It's almost the same except the family views the body for the last time before being seated,"

"How long is the service?"

"Tonight, it should only be an hour. But tomorrow it could last two or three hours. Dignitaries at funerals always prolong the time. The Sheriff in Redwood City called and said the police would be there to help with the traffic."

"Detective DeMarcus a reporter asked to interview me. I don't know what to say. Pastor Davenport was an exceptional man. Deacon Hamilton will be with me."

"Rev. Nelson, did you say, Deacon Hamilton?"

"Yes, he's the head of the Deacon Board. He was with Pastor Davenport the night he died. He's such a help." Alfred tried to compose himself, but he could feel that adrenaline rush.

"How long has he been at the church?"

"He and his wife joined about six months ago. He's taking the death of Pastor Davenport hard."

"Do you have his phone number?"

"Yes." Rev. Nelson recited the number.

"Rev. Nelson, please call me if you need any help from me." Alfred hung up.

He knew he had to speak to the deacon before the reporter.

Alfred called Deacon Hamilton and set up a meeting within an hour. Mr. Hamilton hesitated but agreed to meet. Billy had the interview with Melvin Schwarz, so Alfred hurried out the office. Forty-Five minutes later he was knocking on Hamilton's door. A woman answered.

"Hello."

"Hello, I'm Detective DeMarcus." Alfred showed her his badge.

"I called earlier, May I speak with Mr. John Hamilton?" Mrs. Hamilton smiled.

"I'm Mrs. Hamilton; please come in." It was an ordinary house in the suburbs. Mrs. Hamilton was a tall African-American lady with graying hair between 45 and 50 years old. She escorted Alfred into the living room where he met Mr. John Hamilton. Mr. Hamilton was a dark skin man around six feet eight inches tall, who appeared to be in good physical shape. After shaking hands, he offered Alfred a seat on the couch.

"Mr. Hamilton, I'm conducting an investigation regarding the death of Pastor Davenport." The deacon had a surprised look on his face.

"What type of investigation are you talking about?"

"Do you mind if I tape our conversation?" Alfred took a small tape recorder out of his pocket. Hamilton looked uncomfortable but said,

"I guess it's OK." Alfred continued to explain.

"When a prominent member of the community dies we investigate the death to ensure there was no foul play." Hamilton's facial expression changed. He looked perplexed.

"But Pastor Davenport died of a heart attack."

"Yes, I know. I understand you were with Pastor Davenport at the convention." Hamilton hesitated.

"Yes, I was. I can still see the image of Pastor Davenport clutching his chest and falling. It was shocking." Alfred asked,

"What time did you meet with Pastor Davenport before he preached?" Hamilton quickly answered, "No, I got there late. He was already in the pulpit." Alfred continued, "So, you never met him in person that night?"

"No."

"Where were you sitting?"

"I sat in the front row with the other deacons. When he passed out, the preacher's helped him. I wasn't able to get close to him. One of the preachers recognized me and gave me his briefcase. I called Rev. Nelson and told him what happened. By then, Pastor Davenport was in the ambulance. I called my wife. We decided to drive his car home. I knew Rev. Nelson would contact Sister Davenport so we didn't go to the hospital. I left the keys with the maid, and we came home."

"Who told you he died?"

"Rev. Nelson called me that night. It was such a shock. I still can't believe it."

"When you talked to him earlier did he sound like he was having any problems?"

"No Detective."

"Thank you for seeing me on such short notice." Alfred gave him a business card and left. In the car, he had that gut feeling, but he didn't know why. He went back to the office.

In the meantime, Billy was interviewing Melvin Schwarz. According to him, Gail Davenport was his best friend. Melvin was adamant he didn't have any enemies. He talked to Gail Monday before he died. Gail asked him to donate money to the church building fund. He agreed to give him $50,000. Melvin remembered Gail dating Carolyn Johnson. He said she was possessive and jealous which is why he ended the relationship. Gail was devastated when she told him about the pregnancy. He swore he never slept with her, but the paternity test proved he was the father. Gail bought her a house and paid the medical bills, but she still made his life a living hell. The more he gave, the more she wanted. She threatened to tell his wife about the child. He was going to tell Yolanda and pray she forgave him for not telling her sooner."

After speaking with Melvin, Billy had a better feeling about Carolyn Johnson and it wasn't good.

Alfred brought lunch back to the office. They shared information and decided they needed to call the Dallas Police. Lieutenant Radar called his counterpart in Dallas who assigned a detective to assist in the investigation. Minutes later, a Deputy Commander Burk called. Alfred asked if he had any information on Carolyn Johnson. The Commander said he'd check and call them back.

Alfred walked out of the office and called Evelyn.

"Hello."

"Hello, Alfred. You sound tired."

"I have to tell you; this case is getting to me."

"I'm sorry to hear that. Is there anything I can do to help?"

"No Evelyn, this is just one of those tough cases. I am going to close it."

"I know you will. I'm praying for you. I'll see you tonight." Alfred hung up.

Chapter 31

Thursday morning Yolanda woke up crying. She hardly slept. The service for her husband is today. Yolanda's been trying to get used to being a widow. The love of her life was never coming home. Today, his body would be viewed by strangers. It was hard to accept that he had a child. Melvin called and said he talked to Gail a few weeks before he passed and that he was planning to tell her about the child. Melvin asked Yolanda to forgive Gail posthumously. He said Carolyn trapped Gail into being a father. Yolanda started to think about what Melvin said. She showered and went downstairs.

Doris prepared breakfast. Yolanda's parents and brother were eating. No one knew how she would react. The past few days, Yolanda had been erratic, but under the circumstances, they accepted it. The family was on edge. At home, it was family, but in public, Yolanda would be severely judged for how she acted. They were afraid Carolyn Johnson would show up, and Yolanda would lose it.

"Good morning, everyone," they all responded. Yolanda's face looked haggard. She wasn't sleeping.

"Sweetheart, did you get any sleep?"

"No, Mother. I think I'm going to take one of those sleeping pills tonight."

"Are you sure that's a good idea. You don't want to fall asleep during the service tomorrow. Why don't you take a nap? I'll call you in time to get dressed."

"Thanks, Mother." Yolanda poured herself a cup of coffee, turned and went upstairs to bed.

All calls on Yolanda's house phones were forwarded to the phone service and Yolanda's dad was checking the report. Carolyn hadn't called again. A reporter requested an interview. Attorney Mark Benson was asked to respond.

Ray was quiet all week. He was concerned about his sister. His feelings toward his dead brother-in-law were mixed. He couldn't decide if Gail was a good man or a lying dog.

The Davenport's called and agreed to meet at six o'clock. The funeral home limo would arrive at six-thirty in time to get them all to the church by seven o'clock. Everyone returned to their rooms.

Chapter 32

Carolyn Johnson is a strong, angry woman. Her mother was a single parent. Growing up, they lived in the rough part of town which gave Carolyn street toughness. She was the bully on the block. But her grades didn't reflect her attitude. Going to college seemed to soften her. She wanted to be a doctor. When she met Gail, it gave her hope for a better future. She'd been trying to talk to his attorney, but he wouldn't return her calls.

So to get even with him and add insult to injury she decided to attend Gail's funeral even though it was against her mother's wishes. Carolyn decided her son Michael should see his grandparents. She felt it was time for the world to know the truth. Her flight arrived in Oakland Thursday at 2:00 p.m. She rented a car and checked into the hotel. The message on the church phone said the service started at seven. She was going.

Carolyn dated Gail for months; then he dumped her for Yolanda. She decided to make him pay. It wasn't hard to drug him. She wanted him, but he kept saying he was saving himself for marriage, but she knew what to do. As a med student, she knew how to get semen. The look on his face was precious when she told him she was pregnant. Even without a paternity test, she knew the kid was his. As far as she was concerned dying wouldn't absolve his family from paying her child support for life.

At the Oakland Police Station Alfred and Billy were working hard. Alfred dialed Amy's number, and she answered.

"Hello, Amy, this is Detective DeMarcus."

"Detective, why are you calling me?"

"Amy, in my hand I'm holding Rev. Davenport's phone. Can you guess what I found?"

"Are you talking about my text messages?"

"That's what I'm talking about."

"Detective, I'm sorry. I'm sorry. I had a crush on Pastor Davenport. I'm ashamed. I asked him to delete my texts, but I guess he didn't. Mrs. Davenport found out and fired me. I don't blame her. I don't know what I was thinking."

"When was the last time you saw Pastor Davenport?"

"It was a month ago."

"Are you sure?"

"Yes, Detective, I'm sure."

"If you're lying, I'll have you picked up. Do you understand?" He asked with a stern voice.

"Yes Sir. I'm not lying."

"Goodbye." He hung up.

Alfred believed her. The last text from her on Gail's phone was over a month old. He took her off the suspect list.

Billy was working with Adam, the clerk that was helping them. They were still comparing membership lists trying to find similarity. Only a few names matched and they were elderly members. He looked at the homeowners again. There was no evidence to keep Avis Daniels as a suspect. He eliminated her from the list. Alfred called Carolyn Johnson, but there was no answer.

The Detective's list of suspects was getting shorter. They still didn't know why Gail Davenport died.

Alfred and Billy arrived at the church two hours before service began. They wanted to survey the area. The church and parking lot were huge. An area was cordoned off for dignitaries and family. Inside the church, the casket lay across the pulpit area. Flowers covered the area and lined the outer aisles. Billy checked the position of the cameras while Alfred met members of the Redwood City Police officers. Across the street from the church was a news truck from a local TV station. Lieutenant Radar called to tell him the Mayor of Oakland would attend tonight's service. The Redwood City Mayor would attend the funeral tomorrow. Alfred had a feeling Carolyn would show up. He had her picture sent to police officers phones. An hour later the church was filling up. A reporter interviewed attendees as they came in. One approached Billy, but he gave the standard answer, no comment. By the time the service would start the church would be packed. Alfred and Billy stationed themselves in front of the church.

At 6:15 he got word that Carolyn Johnson and her son were in the building. Billy spotted her first. She walked down the middle aisle straight to the casket wearing a black dress with shades and red hair. The little boy wore a little blue suit and bow tie. He looked like Gail and everyone took notice. There was no mistaking her intention. She stood in front of the open casket for almost one minute then turned walked back down the middle aisle and took a seat behind where the family would be sitting. The murmuring in the church was loud. Some people took pictures, and so did the detectives. Thirty-five minutes later everyone was asked to stand while the family came in.

Yolanda wore a black silk suit with a large black hat covered by a veil with sunglasses. She looked eloquent. Surrounding her was her brother, parents and Mr. and Mrs. Davenport, followed by a security team. The family sat down followed by the congregation. Billy moved to the wall aisle close to Carolyn. Service proceeded with Rev. Nelson in charge. Alfred saw Evelyn walk in. She sat in the section near him. Their eyes met, and he smiled. An hour later, Rev. Nelson asked everyone to remain seated while the family exited. The service was over.

Alfred made it a point to follow Carolyn Johnson to her car. She was surprised when he stopped her. Alfred introduced himself. He asked to speak to her privately. She became irate. To avoid causing a scene, he told her he would meet her at six p.m., the following day. Alfred and Billy drove back to the office.

Meanwhile, in the limousine, Yolanda became hysterical. Her father called the doctor and had him meet them at the house. Both Yolanda and Gail's mother were given a sedative and put to bed. Ray retreated to his bedroom. The fathers sat in the library feeling helpless.

"Thurston, what are we going to do? I don't think Yolanda or your wife will survive this."

"I wish I knew. I think I saw that Carolyn woman at the service."

"What?"

"I didn't want to say it in front of the women. But there was this woman with red hair that looked like Gail's old girlfriend."

"My God, are you sure?" He began pacing. "Yolanda can't take it. I'm calling the police." He dialed Alfred's number.

"Hello."

"Hello, Detective DeMarcus, this is Mr. Morris. Thurston Davenport and I were talking. He thinks he saw that Carolyn woman at church. I need you to stop her from coming."

"Mr. Morris, I understand your feelings, but she has every right to be there. It isn't breaking the law to attend a funeral."

"So, you saw her, too?

"I did. I'm meeting with her tomorrow."

"I don't want that woman near my daughter and if you can't protect her, I will." He slammed the phone down.

Alfred told Billy about the call.

"Man, I don't know this chick, but I don't like her myself." They laughed.

"Tomorrow, let's have a surveillance camera put inside the sanctuary. Al, where was Hamilton?"

"I don't know. I'll call Houston P.D., and see if they have anything on this guy."

At the office, Alfred called the Houston Police Department and asked if they had any information on John Hamilton. A Detective Wilson said he'd check and call him back. While waiting, they went over the information the Dallas Police sent.

Ten minutes later Detective Wilson called and said he had nothing on John Hamilton. Alfred read him the SSN again. Detective Wilson gave him the same answer. There was no information on a John Hamilton. Detective Wilson asked Alfred if he had a picture of the guy.

Alfred was puzzled. He told the detective he would call him back.

Billy checked Facebook. There were no pictures of the Hamilton's. Billy told Alfred. He watched as Alfred stood up, grabbed his coat and headed for the door. Billy knew what that meant; he was mad. Billy grabbed his jacket and followed. In the car, Billy texted the number and an error message popped up, "invalid number." Alfred put the siren on while Billy called the Palo Alto Police and asked for their assistant and back up. Thirty minutes later a patrol car was waiting outside of the Hamilton residence. Alfred knocked on the door, but the house was dark. Billy walked around to the back of the house. No one answered. Alfred explained the situation to the patrol officers. A few minutes later Palo Alto Detectives arrived. Alfred called Lieutenant Radar and they called their Lieutenant. Everyone agreed. It was important to get in that house. While waiting for a subpoena Billy and Alfred canvassed the neighborhood. No one knew the Hamilton's or saw them leave.

An hour later a subpoena was signed, and they entered the house. There was no sign of foul play. Everything seemed in order, but there was a heavy odor of cleaning fluid. There were no pictures and no house phone. Clothes were in the closet but there was no food in the refrigerator. In the back yard, Billy found a BBQ grill with evidence of a recent burn. They didn't find a credit card receipt, a bill, or anything, but the cell phone that was turned off, and left on the kitchen table. These people vanished. The Palo Alto Detectives called the CSI techs and asked them to process the house. The only thing missing were the residents and their car.

Alfred called and asked for a reconstructive artist to meet him in the office. Billy and Alfred drove back to Oakland leaving the CSI tech at work. They knew they had to find these people.

Alfred gave the artist enough information to make a composite sketch. Billy put out an APB identifying the Hamilton's as persons of interest.

Alfred checked on the police AFAS system, but no one resembled John or Beth Hamilton if that's who they were. Alfred sent a copy of the sketch to the Houston Police Department. The Houston detective said he'd call if he found anything.

It was after midnight, Alfred and Billy went home exhausted and more determined than ever to solve this murder.

Chapter 33

Early Friday morning, Attorney Mark Benson was in his office. The night before, he received a call from two angry fathers. They told him to get in touch with Carolyn Johnson and offer her two million dollars to stay away from the funeral and their families. Benson set up a meeting with her for 9:00 a.m. And he wasn't looking forward to it.

Mark Benson arrived at the hotel early. Carolyn was angry. She even threatened to hurt the attorney if he woke up her son sleeping on the bed. He introduced himself and presented the offer. He was expecting her to yell and throw things. Instead, she just sat there and listened. Without a word, she grabbed the check, stuck it in her bra and told him to get out. She refused to sign a receipt, so he left. Benson called Mr. Morris and told him what happened.

Alfred and Billy were in the office before 7:00 a.m. The Hamilton's were still missing. The APB hadn't resulted in finding them. They were on the run. Alfred thought about calling Evelyn but didn't. He had too much on his mind.

Billy called the Dallas Police, but they had nothing on John or Beth Hamilton. CSI didn't find any usable fingerprints at the Hamilton house. Alfred and Billy drove to the church. The Redwood City Police force was visible everywhere. Lieutenant Radar met them at a side entrance. Alfred gave him an update. Alfred couldn't believe it. Radar gave them a contact in the FBI. Alfred called the FBI contact who told him to send the sketch to him.

Several ministers and their wives arrived in the dedicated parking area. The Redwood City Mayor came with his entourage. At 10:45 a.m. Carolyn Johnson arrived. She and her son wore black which made her red hair very noticeable. Again, Carolyn walked down the middle aisle to the casket. After standing motionless for a few seconds, Carolyn picked up her son, placed an envelope in the dead man's hand and walked away. The funeral director immediately retrieved it and put it in his pocket. This time, she sat near the back of the church. Except for the music, you could hear a pin drop.

The Family was late. Everyone remained seated. Ministers and security guards surrounded the family as they entered. Gail's parents viewed the body first. Yolanda's parents were next, which left Ray holding Yolanda's hand. Two ministers joined them as Yolanda walked to the casket. To everyone's surprise, Yolanda stared at the man she loved, then bent over and kissed him. Some of the women began crying. It was if they knew how she felt. With her head held high, Yolanda walked to the pew and sat down without any assistance. Ray sat next to her, held her hand and whispered how proud he was of her. They closed the casket and placed flowers over it. Rev. Nelson began. Two hours later, the songs, talks, and sermon were over. The casket of Rev. Gail Davenport rolled down the middle aisle followed by ministers, the family, and security team. The family sat quietly in the limos, and Carolyn Johnson disappeared.

Billy gathered up the surveillance footage while Alfred waited. As he turned to leave, a minister approached him who he recognized from the convention.

"Detective DeMarcus"

"Yes."

"I'm Rev. Calloway." They shook hands.

"It's nice to meet you, Rev. Calloway. How can I help you?"

"I was just talking to Ms. Jenkins about Pastor Davenport. She said I should tell you Deacon Hamilton asked me to give a cold bottle of water to Pastor Davenport before he was to speak the night he died."

Alfred held his face still and tried not to show how shocked he was.

Rev. Calloway continued.

"I don't know what that means, but maybe you do." It took him a few seconds to realize what happened.

"Yes, Yes I do. Thank you, Pastor, thank you. Alfred knew that meant the bottle of water placed near Gail was the poison. He looked around for Evelyn, but she had gone. He told Billy everything in the car.

"What the Hell? That's it." He shouted.

They drove to the grave site. The only people at the grave site were ministers, the family, and about thirty church members. Carolyn was a no show.

It was five o'clock when they left the cemetery. Alfred was anxious to speak with Carolyn Johnson. He drove directly to the hotel. The desk clerk said she'd checked out two hours earlier. They asked to see the room. Diapers, food wrappers, and trash were the only things they found. The clerk gave them the license plate of the car. Billy called Carolyn's cell, but it went straight to voicemail. He left a message and put out an APB on the car. Now two primary suspects were missing, and they were from Texas. Alfred and Billy knew they found the killers.

Alfred called Lieutenant Radar gave him an update. Radar authorized them to fly to Texas. There were still no results from the APB's. They packed and met at the airport.

During the flight, Alfred called Evelyn.

"Hello."

"Hello stranger."

His voice dropped low and sexy.

"I deserved that. Thank you for steering Rev. Calloway to me. You won't believe all that has happened in the last 24 hours. I was so glad to see you at the service. I just couldn't get close enough to kiss those beautiful brown lips." There was silence on the phone.

"Alfred, I realize your job is 24/7. I'm just concerned that you don't need to be in a relationship." He felt his heart skip a beat.

His voice was somber as he continued.

"Evelyn, you have no idea how much I want to be with you. Meeting you has changed my life. You mean so much to be. Please before you dump me, let's talk in person."

"Can you come over now?"

"Baby, I wish I could, but I'm on a plane headed for Texas."

"When you get back, give me a call." Click

Alfred took a deep breath and put the phone in his pocket. Billy pretended not to listen. He put the earphones in his ear and watched TV. As sad as he felt, Alfred knew he had to concentrate on this case. Billy called the office. TSA reported that Carolyn boarded a plane to Dallas hours after the funeral.

"So what's the plan, big guy?"

"Let's talk to the detective who sent the information. Then, I'll talk to Carolyn."

"Sounds like a plan. There's still no word on the APB for the Hamilton's."

"Billy, I've been thinking, what if Carolyn and the Hamilton's are related?"

Alfred called ahead and asked Detective Wilson to check for relatives of Carolyn Johnson. Billy called Houston P.D. and asked for the same information.

It was late when Billy and Alfred arrived in Dallas Texas. After getting a rental car, they checked in to a hotel. The Detectives felt they were nearing the end of this investigation.

Early Saturday morning Alfred and Billy drove to the Dallas Police Department. They met Detective Wilson who gave them a list of known relatives. Based on the background check several had records for shoplifting, robbery, and petty larceny. Alfred and Billy spent most of the day looking at mud shots. As Alfred looked at the rap sheets, a picture of Earl Harrison caught his eye. Staring at him was Earl Harrison of Austin, Texas better known to Alfred as John Hamilton.

"Got you." Alfred shouted.

He called Lieutenant Radar who agreed to contact the Austin Police and ask for their help. Alfred and Billy drove to the address of Carolyn Johnson. Instead of knocking on the door they decided to park in the neighborhood and just observe. Sure enough within thirty minutes, Carolyn emerged from the house carrying her son. Her hair was dyed black and she looked like a typical young mother. They followed her to another residence where an older woman met her at the door. With both addresses in hand, they decided it was more important to question the Hamilton's AKA the Harrison's before confronting Carolyn. The Dallas police put a surveillance team on her, so there was no way she was getting away.

That evening after contacting the Austin Police, Alfred and Billy drove the two and a half hours to Austin, Texas. They gathered as much information as they could on the Harrisons. They had extensive records from assault with a deadly weapon, assault, and battery, insurance fraud to extortion. Even though they were arrested, they never served any jail time. The victims refused to testify against them, so the assault charges were dropped. They lived in a high crime area well-known for gang activity. The Harrison's instilled fear in anyone who dared cross their path.

With help from the gang unit of the Austin Police Billy and Alfred formulated a plan. They obtained warrants for the arrest of the Harrisons for first-degree murder. With the help from the Austin Swat team at 3:00 a.m. Sunday morning, the Harrison house was surrounded. They were captured without an incident.

For hours, Earl Harrison and his wife Melissa were belligerent. But when confronted with the death penalty, Earl asked for a plea deal. He confessed and said his cousin Carolyn hired them to kill Gail Davenport. Carolyn was always telling the family how horrible Gail was to her. She told them he refused to pay child support, so they hated him. Carolyn promised Earl $25,000 to get close to Davenport and another $25,000 when Gail was dead. With both confessions, they would be extradited back to Oakland to stand trial.

Late Sunday night, Alfred and Billy thanked the Austin Police for their help. They drove back to Dallas Texas. They obtained a warrant for Carolyn Johnson. With help from the Dallas Police at 4:00 a.m. Monday morning Alfred rang the bell with his gun drawn.

When the door opened, the look on Carolyn's face said it all.

"Hello, Carolyn, can we talk?"

She was tough but eventually confessed. Carolyn hated Yolanda. She blamed Yolanda for Gail breaking up with her. Carolyn wanted to be Mrs. Davenport, but instead, Gail offered money instead. She provided the poison to the Harrison's. When Gail called Harrison and asked him to meet at the convention, Harrison decided that was the perfect time to spike the water to kill him. Carolyn Johnson was charged with conspiracy and first-degree murder. When told of Carolyn's arrest, her ailing mother had a heart attacked and died. Alfred called Lieutenant Radar and gave him the update. Lieutenant Radar congratulated them.

On Tuesday, Carolyn Johnson, Earl Harrison, and his wife Melissa were all extradited back to Oakland to stand trial for the murder of Rev. Gail Davenport.

After taking a seat on the plane Billy said.

"Al, I never imagined us running around Texas arresting killers for an Oakland crime. I called my mother, she's so proud." He laughed.

"Billy, you know us, we'll go to the end of the earth to catch a killer" They both laughed.

When Alfred and Billy landed at the Oakland Airport, they were tired but satisfied with how they closed the case.

The mayor set up a press conference for the following day.

Even though they were tired, Alfred and Billy wanted to update the family in person before the news media leaked any information. Billy called en route. He asked that the whole family be present. Yolanda agreed. Everyone was waiting in the library. They even had their attorney on speaker phone.

Alfred gave them an update on the case. Everyone was stunned. It brought tears to their eyes. Mr. Morris was the first to speak.

"Detectives, first let me say thank you for your dedication and hard work. These last weeks have been the hardest we've ever had. My son-in-law was a gift from God. He wasn't perfect, but he loved my daughter, and he will be missed." Yolanda interrupted.

"What my dad is trying to tell you is that you have reinforced our love for Gail and God. He tried to make the best of a bad situation. The day of the funeral I could feel his spirit with me. That's the only way I was able to find strength to endure the funeral. I feel his spirit with me now. I'm no longer afraid to live without him." Attorney Benson spoke.

Detectives I also want to thank you. For the record, the family gave Ms. Johnson a check for two million dollars. At the funeral, she put it in the casket. The funeral director retrieved it for us. I think she was expecting to extort money for a long time. The detectives were surprised.

"Thank you for telling us. That proves this was not about money."

"Detectives, what's going to happen to the child?" Yolanda asked.

"I believe Child Services is placing him in a foster home." She gasped and turned to the family.

"I think I speak for everyone." They all nodded in approval. "We want to adopt him. He's an innocent child. He's Gail's son and their grandchild. We can give him the lifestyle Gail wanted and plenty of love."

"Mrs. Davenport, you're a kind lady. I'm sure your attorney can make that happen." Everyone agreed.

Family members hugged them as they left. Walking to the car, Billy said, "Al, I must say this has been a wild ride."

"I agree."

When they walked in the office, co-workers gave them a standing ovation. Alfred and Billy appreciated it but they too tired to care.

Alfred felt like the weight of the world was lifted off his shoulders. All he could think about was Evelyn. Alfred DeMarcus drove to the travel agency. Deborah was the first person he saw.

"Hello, Detective." she smiled.

"Hello, Deborah. Is she in?"

"Yes but I don't think she wants to see you."

"Let me be the judge of that." Alfred smiled and walked past her. He entered Evelyn's office without knocking and closed the door behind him. She was surprised to see him. Alfred walked around her desk, grabbed her by the waist, forced his body tight against hers and passionately kissed her. Evelyn's knees went weak, and her body responded. He whispered in her ear.

"I want you now!" He took her hand; she grabbed her purse, and they walked out the office hand in hand.